MW01002831

Thank you to the support.
I hope you enjoy the novel,
Please don't hesitate to
reach out with your
thoughts @Real Marco Cavazos

M.

WORD REBELS PRESS

Word Rebels L.L.C.
506 N. Bishop Ave
Dallas, TX 75208
wordrebels.com

ISBN:
978-1-7366205-1-9

Library of Congress Control Number:
2023903955

Printed in Texas
United States of America

NAKED GULLS

A NOVEL

MARCO CAVAZOS

@RealMarcoCavazos

1.

It looks like a giant banana, but it's a ton of bread floating in the ocean. I guess that's the Indian. It's got to be the Indian. I've never seen anything like it, and the Indian's the only ocean I've never seen. But then again, who can tell oceans apart? The gulls won't touch it, the bread, not even the naked ones, the ones with no feathers, sad eyes, sunburn. They linger, fixated on the loaf as it rises and falls in the surf, while the feathered birds circle above in figure eights. They swoosh in, glide out like bombers.

All of this from my balcony window, sitting at a desk in some secret hotel. The view is mostly ocean, but there's an angle where I can catch a glimpse of two of the pool loungers. I wonder if that shadow is Sonia Salazar, then I look again to the sea. There's something dancing out there on the island or maybe there's not. It's pretty foggy.

The water is black, but green starts to show. The sun wants to come up from somewhere beyond the horizon, un-

5

der the cloud cover, but she's as stuck as I am. Maybe it's the rhythm, the routine, the rising every day setting every night that's driving her crazy. Congestion on the cosmic highway? Pollution clouds hiding the Earthlings from mother's warmth?

Sidenote: I thought about calling this novel *Banana Island*, then I considered *Gulls*, *The Gulls*, *Warhol's Birds*, and finally *Naked Gulls*. I'm still not convinced it's the way to go, but we'll stick with it for now. Not that you can do anything about it. Plus, this book and its title only matter if anything can matter.

Morning. There's that smell, that twilight. The bodily aches from a long night, the need to piss, gunk build-up in my mouth, thirst... blurry vision, pondering whether or not that taste in my dream was something I ate in my sleep (a spider?).

My glow-parrot is getting tired. On the first night, I had two, one blue and one red. Last night, the desk only sent one. He's a beautiful green though, just tired. The green light was hard to write by, but the words didn't come off angry like they did with the red glow-parrot. The surprising thing about glow-parrots is how glasslike they are when they're positioned on a light fixture and how evenly their radiance glows.

"The sun's coming up," I say. "Get some rest." I open the door, and he flys away.

I push the welcome fruit basket towards the end of the desk, and I load an A4 into the Underwood to jot some notes on the silhouettes of the normal, feathered gulls turning figure eights in the twilight, how the now rising sun's orange-gray-blue filter gives the bread-island thing a mountainy quality, how the birds are quiet except for a few naked gulls dipping their beaks into a communal pot of what has to be coffee.

I crumple up the A4, throw it away, and load a fresh sheet.

I also considered *Banana Bread* for a title.

We're staying in a secret hotel designed by Andy Warhol as a side project sometime in the late sixties, so I'm told. Repeatedly. This place is super fucking weird. That sort of intentional, cringey weird. A weird-by-design weird ostensibly inspired by the absurdity of human existence pushing the extremes of style and behavior to our cultural limits. There's an orgy floor, a smoker's garden, an ocean-water rooftop pool, and an extravagant build-it-yourself ice cream bar with coconut shell bowls and topping options that include illegal unpasteurized chocolate varieties. I might be visiting it in my sleep, but this will go unaddressed from here.

My purpose here is questionable at best. I'm attending at Mr. Delivan's insistence, invited, more like summoned, last minute in formal business language by e-mail. In addition to Mr. Delivan, I'm joined by an inventor called Eduardo Ruiz, the journalist Sonia Salazar, and Mr. Delivan's associate Ed White. That's why I keep saying "we" about stuff. I guess that's obvious, whatever.

I saw Ed White when he dropped by with an itinerary, but that's it. It looked like this:

Morning: Meet & Greet Breakfast in the Smoker's Garden

Mid-Morning: Dr. Ruiz's Presentation

Rest of Day: TBD

I'm dying to meet Sonia Salazar. I've held this off for about as long as I can. I stand up to check on the shadows of the pool loungers. They're gone.

Jesus Christ I'm dying to meet her.

Hell, this might be what's behind my insomnia (or nausea? Hey, Jean-Paul), my inability to type any keepers, the thrashing, the dreams (or nightmares), the hallucinations (or visions). Maybe it's better to keep my idealized notions within my imagination, in their black and white photographs—but no one would refuse a chance to meet Sonia Salazar.

She was on Letterman once. As far as I know, she's been the only person besides Berrymore to make him blush. They wouldn't let her on King. Her answers were too wordy for quick format news.

I type "Dear Sonia," pounding out the details of the life we'd have together, memories of seeing her on TV, with some isn't-it-funny-you-were-my-celebrity-crush-and-now-look-at-us type jokes, and "yo, don't be creepy" six times in a row.

Crumple. Trash can. Un-crumple. Lighter, ashtray.

My room overlooks the water, the sky, an endless expanse of sea that turns gray and dead when you gaze into her vastitude but bright green when you blink towards her soul. I'm on the twenty-ninth floor, "Split Pea." Yeah, the floors are soup can names.

The doorman posted outside my suite will attend to my every whim and desire, but I've been inclined not to partake in the use of his services. He clears his throat 24/7, his leather creaks every time he bends to check his boot polish, and the rustle from when he brushes away lint from his hot pink wool uniform (the fashion vibe here seems straight out of Zoolander) is like a mosquito or cricket in your ear.

I can't sleep. I can't fucking sleep, and maybe it's not Sonia Salazar. Maybe it's this, all this, this trap, the way our feet are glued to this planet no matter how hard we try to jump, the way time dances around us, laughing and mocking us for our inability to get it. The more I can't sleep, the more I think sleep might be the answer to everything. The world could be a wonderful place if everyone got a full night's sleep. Nah, that's cheesy.

Despite the view (it's breathtaking if you forget about the floating bread, which must really stink up close), the welcome fruit basket I haven't touched yet (apples, oranges, a mango, a jackfruit, a pomegranate, some mini bananas, a package of mixed nuts), the twenty-four hour personal doorman standing at attention (asshole), clean white sheets, new pillows, every luxury considered, you guessed it:

I. can't. fucking. sleep.

And get this. My room has no bathroom, but Mr. Deli-

9

van has paid for everything, so shhh. No bathroom. In a suite. It's some sick art joke Warhol must have thought up on one of those pretentious benders with that creepy half smile.

When I have to go, I use the one in the lobby. Bladder full? lobby. Bowels full? lobby. Think the bladder might be full pretty soon and you want to sleep for a while? lobby. And, now that I'm thinking about it—lobby.

The whole thing's killed my van-life ambitions. Fuck, man. All those hours on YouTube for nothing. I guess the saving grace is that I got to figure it out now, vanlessly, rather than by driving around at 3am looking for a public bathroom, considering a bucket, and cursing my own damn self for poor life choices masked as minimalist naturalist ambition.

Maybe I'm just getting older, maybe it's this stupid situation, but I find myself having to urinate three times before bed every night. Once before I get in bed, again when I finish reading (I'm reading *Rich Dad, Poor Dad*. Kidding. Screw that entire genre. I'm reading Sartre's *Nausea* again. Maybe that's why I can't sleep.), and for a third time just after I start dozing. This wakes me up, and I end up drinking water to clear the sleep goo out of my mouth, which basically starts the routine all over.

Only now, the fat front-desk boy, Pudge Johnson (real name unknown, but it's probably something overly fancy to the point of being idiotic. I suspect "Henry James William George Marshall Donnovan III"), has come up with this schedule, printed out and taped inside the door, for bathroom privileges like I'm overindulging. The kid's got to be something like 15, and he's the boss. My 200-year-old doorman cowers around the kid.

And, me, I have to sneak by him just to use the bathroom. He's getting wise. He's on the lookout. I heard him whispering to my doorman, something like "*pst pst pst* if he *pst pst* bathroom *pst pst…*" but I'm not worried about it. The doorman may be useless and an asshole, but goddamn he's loyal. Loyal like a dog though. Like, he's always there. He's happy to see me. He may not have any real idea what's going on.

I twist the knob, the latch pops echoing down the hall, and the doorman snaps his heels.

"Laundry, sir?"

"No, thanks, I'm just—"

"Some room service, sir?"

"No, thanks again. I'm—"

"Is something bothering you? Harassing phone calls?"

"No, no, I—"

"We've had a problem lately with harassing phone calls. If that's the issue, it's quite alright to tell me. We suspect a competing hotel, between you and I, sir."

"No, no phone calls. I'm—"

"It's quite alright for us to have secrets, you and I. That's why I filled you in on the harassing phone calls bit. We can agree to keep such intrigue quiet." He winks. "What can I do for you, sir?"

"Nothing, thank you. God." I'm in my complimentary cotton velour slippers, matching sky blue robe. "Why are you blocking me?" I shove past. As much as I like him, he does need an elbow now and then. Like how some people might do with a dog. Not in a mean way, of course. In a training-not-to-jump-on-me way.

"Oof."

"Did he put you up to this? Pudge. Did he? That son of a bitch. Let me tell you something, if I ever get on Yelp, his name's gonna be all over that 1 star."

"Up to what, sir? I thought we were in a moment. Were we not in a moment? Just now, about the phone calls?"

"I'm going now." I feel slow and heavy. I picture myself looking like Tony Soprano when he goes to the fridge for snacks in his pajamas. Am I allowed to name HBO characters? It's like music sampling, right? I think I'm alright as long as I don't say something like Tony Soprano was staying in the room across from me with the goomah from season two and he said… etc. That I can't do. Unless that's fanfiction? Anyway, it doesn't matter. I feel like fat hungry Tony, that's the point.

My slippers drag against the blonde shag rug that runs the hall. It has hot pink walls, blonde accents, and disco-ball-inspired fixtures. I pass by doors to lifeless, silver-painted rooms (I've seen the doors open) guarded by more statuesque doormen in similarly pink uniforms.

Probably haunted, this place. The paint color is more aluminum foil than silver, but you get the idea. Random

12

candles light the hall, dripping wax to form wax stalagmites doing a number on the carpet. All the light in the hotel is either natural or from a candle, reflected by disco balls. I find the candles un-Warhol, and, frankly, I suspect the hotel is a forgery or some other kind of twisted art joke.

Actually, it's a commentary on materialism. I get it, Warhol. We're paying (well, Mr. Delivan is paying) the premium to stay all 5 star, and you're over there reminding us that luxury isn't everything. That we're supposed to take in and appreciate the flickering candles at night and the UV heating up our lounge chairs by day. The candlelit disco balls though, alright, I'll give him that, they're cool.

I pass the doormen, and each offers their service with the snapping of heels. "Thank you." "No, thank you." "I'm fine, thank you," I say.

The vibe mellows in the elevator where the call buttons are Campbell's Soup cans. I take a minute to try to remember the soup for the lobby. Cream of Mushroom? But that takes me up. It's Turkey Noodle, that's right, and Pepper Pot is the Smoker's Garden.

Pudge Johnson, working the desk with a look like he'd been waiting for me, blocks my path with the shuffle step that accompanies the *this way, sir* of a non-consensual politically motivated van entry (Like when the CIA takes someone for a meeting or something, get it?)

"What?"

"Sir?"

"Why are you looking at me like that? I need to go." I

try to pass. He steps back, angles to block me again.

"It's your third time today. We have other guests."

"Don't start with me, Pudge. How's that your business? Move."

"It's specifically my business. You've been three times today." He looks over his shoulder towards the front desk where the brass key hangs from a hook. The key itself dangles from a length of white cord tethered to a section of 2 x 4 about a foot long like they have at gas stations. "I've personally taken ownership of this case."

"I don't have a bathroom in my room. This is a customer service problem. It's my first time today. Your job is to provide customer service. Look, I get it. You're an art hotel. It's all a statement. I get it. Something about consumerism or socialism or whatever, but I'm not playing along. Not when I'm paying for it."

"Your stay comes compliments of Mr. Delivan."

"Regardless, I'm a paying customer, Pudge."

"Mr. Delivan—"

"Goddammit, Pudge."

"I have you down at 2:02." He checks a pocket notebook. "Then again at 5:27, making this your—"

"Give me the key. I've been up all night. I want to sleep. How am I going to sleep when I've got to piss?"

"Alright, let's not turn this into a scene. Will you be long? We have other guests." He snaps three times through his white gloves at the skinny boy, Sticks (also not his real name, but his is probably something super normal).

14

Sticks hesitatingly steps away from some paperwork to bring the key. It's messy paperwork, and if I had to guess, completely useless. Pages to be organized, filed, cabinet-boxed just in case the Man comes for a next-level audit, and never looked at again.

"Can you limit yourself to three minutes?"

"That's none of your business," I say.

"Sir, it's specifically my business. As I've said, I've made this my personal case." I reach for the key. "Please, sir, allow me." He bows. The key clicks into the hole under a silver knob. Pudge stands aside, gesturing forward, then he follows me in. "I'm afraid it's specifically my business. May I take your robe?"

"Yes, thank you. I'll be awhile. Maybe you can come back?" I hurry further in, past the first small room. It's a waiting room of sorts with two sculpted disco-ball-textured functional-art armchairs. One is an homage to an elephant, the other a giraffe. The trunk and neck are the respective seats of the designs. There's a lime green shag rug on the floor and white accent tables. The door to the actual toilets is a full length mirror, as if it were a speakeasy. The sinks are also in the first room. I open the mirror door with Pudge close on my tail, get into a stall, and I yank the door shut.

I take a moment to appreciate the green velvet wall linings, and wonder about how they avoid vandalism and keep it clean.

"I must wait," Pudge says, voice muffled like his face is pressed against the outside of the stall door.

A muted knocking.

"You know what, forget it. I'll come back later."

"Sir?"

"Call me a car. I think I'll go into town."

"There are no cars. The hotel is… discreet."

"Okay, well how do I get out of here?"

"Mr. Delivan has arranged everything. If you don't mind, it is almost time for breakfast. The others are waiting in the Smoker's Garden."

"I see."

"Your place is being set now."

"In that case, send for a cigar and a latte. Will you make sure my place is across from Miss Salazar?"

"The seating map was submitted by Mr. Delivan. Everything's been arranged."

"Just the cigar and latte, then."

"I will relay your request, sir."

"I'll be just a second." I stare into the commode. The water is green like the ocean. I try to pee, but nothing comes out. The sensation is overwhelming. I'm thirsty too.

"Not yet? Sir? Almost done?"

"Will you wait outside?"

"I'll write you in for a 9:30, stall three. Now I'm afraid you must go to the Smoker's Garden. At this point, I must insist." I hear the press of a button. The water rotates, then disappears.

I can't go. I can't sleep. I need water.

The whole world is a treadmill that rolls under us. The

16

whole time we're actually just staying in one place. All movement in space or time is pure illusion. It's a giant cage, a hamster wheel. We only feel like we're moving.

"Can you have someone get that bread out of the ocean?" I ask, fitting my robe back on. "I'm worried it smells. I'm worried that smell's going to get into my room."

"The one that looks like a banana, sir?"

"No, the other one."

"I've only seen the banana one."

"Hmm. Well then I guess that one, huh?"

"I don't see how that's any of your business," he says.

"It's disgusting."

"I'm afraid it must stay there for the gulls."

"The gulls won't touch it."

"They will eventually. When they get hungry, sir." Pudge steps back and sits in the elephant chair. He lights a cigarette. "It's a shame, really. A damn shame."

"You're allowed to smoke on duty?" The faucet knob squeaks as I turn it to start washing up, fighting the urge not to drink from the tap like a kid. "Can you make sure I have a bottle of water at breakfast?"

"I don't work here. I'm a volunteer."

"I see. Well, that's nice of you. What is it, like, court mandated?"

"We're all volunteers."

"That makes sense. I get it. There's a restaurant back home that only hires kids out of juvie. Sort of a rehab type thing."

"It's not like that, sir. We're artists."

"You must've made the elephant chair?"

"I wish, sir. It's a Michelangelo."

"Of course, the lost sculpture from his Roman disco period." I shake my hands off. *Screw it*, I think. *I'm too thirsty.* I twist open the cold knob to full, and I dunk my mouth under, lapping at it like a dog at a summer garden hose.

"My God, sir." Pudge jumps up, dropping his cigarette. "I must insist. I'll—" He starts to fumble with his words. The water is amazing, perfect. It's cold and clean and everything water should be. It smells like an untouched trout stream, and maybe it is tapped from one. I can't drink enough. My thirst won't abate. "I'll—I'm going to call—Security! Security!"

"Calm down, Pudge. I'm just rinsing my mouth."

"You have to stop."

"Look." I wipe my mouth off. "The others are waiting. Will you be showing me to the Smoker's Garden?" I move closer. He erects his posture, flustered. I want to hit him, but he's a kid. Surely that's frowned upon here.

"I'm on break. Just press the Pepper Pot can on the elevator. Takes you right to it."

"Thanks, big help. Really big help. Let's call off security maybe? A bit of an overreaction." Really, you can't just up and hit a kid. It's frowned upon in most cultures. Also, he shouldn't be smoking, but that's okay in a lot of places.

"Did you want to add your name to a time slot for a stall?" He's trying to move past the faucet incident. That's amiable of him, but now I'm expecting security to burst in.

"Put me down for the next available," I say. He points to the door with the cigarette he's just picked up from the floor. He's moving right back to the drinking-from-the-faucet thing, you can see it in his eyes. There are little red sparks in there.

"They'll help you at the desk if you can't find the elevator."

"I'm sure they will. How old are you by the way?"

"I'm a volunteer. Close the door, quick. So the smoke doesn't get in the lobby."

"And if I want to check out of here altogether?"

"Go see the desk, then." He shrugs.

I've had it. I'm checking out, finding a proper hotel room with the standard accommodations. As for Mr. Delivan's generosity, that part's easy. I just won't tell him. Or I'll tell him something went wrong at home.

*****

The skinny boy is clacking away on a Remington Portable, his gaze darting between the sheet of paper and the hotel doors. He's hunched over, wearing white gloves tipped with ribbon ink. The bellhop cap reminds me of a Fez hat. It's even got the tassel. Actually, it is a Fez hat. That's got to be another art joke, probably about cultural appropriation.

A man in a gray suit, waiting, catches my eye, saying:

don't waste your time, buddy, this guy's useless. If I had to guess, he'd been there all morning waiting for whatever it was the skinny boy was typing up. I can almost smell the Wite-Out® in the air like when a stranger passes by wearing too much perfume.

So I make my way back to the elevator and press the Pepper Pot can.

2.

Sonia Salazar is naked, but I recognize her right away despite the distraction. She's the living model of that photograph from all my Sunday mornings. I can even smell the coffee, the newspaper ink. I rub my fingers together, and I feel newspaper texture.

The rules here are different, I think.

Someone like Sonia Salazar can be naked, and all of us mortals must bob along pretending she's not. Or pretending that it's fine, that we're fine, that our souls are not on fire and our eyes are not aching from irremissible avoidance in Helen's presence.

Hiding.

Here, in the presence of her nudity, we are the ones who feel naked, exposed, helpless. We feel all the eyes on us.

My beer gut. The crow's feet. The red spot on my forehead. The weird, dry sandpaper spots on Ed White's

21

cheeks.

She's naked.

Smiling. Not really smiling, not grinning, not smirking. It's a flirting smile, a secret smile. The sort of smile that makes whoever sees it think it's for their eyes only. That says *we're sharing a secret. There is an inside joke here. You know me and I know you. It's just us in this world. It's just us laughing at all of this.*

And I grin back.

She's everything her photo promised she would be, but she's missing the black cigarette holder with the gold tip, the eccentric dress, the defiant fashion pieces.

This must be Sonia Salazar in her natural state. This is, afterall, me in my natural state, still in my bathrobe, spa slippers, three-day beard, filled with primal (penile) sensations guiding my judgment—in this case, the urge to pee, pee immediately.

I feel awful. I wonder if she feels awful. I'm presented the way I see myself and the way I hope the world never sees me.

*****

A gull squawks. Mr. Delivan is late, as anyone except for the waiters, apparently, could have predicted. They're letting the hand-chiseled ice sphere melt in his glass at the head of the table. He flew in a special ice man just for the purpose.

The rumor is the ice man's actually an apprentice trav-

22

eling on the sly, that word of his paid ice work could result in serious shame back home, that he's got a pregnant girlfriend, that he's willing to risk the shame because he needs the money for the baby (or the uhm, removal? ambitions unclear). I imagine he's Japanese, but I don't know that, not for a fact. Because of the apprenticeship part, not the abortion thing. I don't know. I'll find out when I see him.

I'm frozen, and they're all watching me. They're performing their choreographed informalities, but I feel their eyes, side glances, quick peeks, radaring ears.

It's a fancy table, by the way. You'd expect vines to climb up its legs in May, flowers in July. It's got a retro vibe, like what I imagine an upper-society English garden party would be like or how the Queen herself might be garden accommodated at a similar hotel.

They have—if I'm going to complain more, I might as well say this—they've decorated the Smoker's Garden with too many exotic plants. So many that the huge leaves look fake, plastic, dated.

The same greenery covers Sonia Salazar. She's wrapped all up in it as though the foliage were blankets and books on a rainy day. Yes, lame. I know. It's an analogy I would only use with someone like Sonia Salazar, who must spend a lot of her time that way.

Nevermind. I'll say it this way instead: she's covered like Eve in a Renaissance oil.

Ed White's doorman, the tallest of them, warms up an accordion standing so close behind Ed's chair that it would be awkward for Ed to leave the table. At the very least, leaving would require a lot of shuffling of positions.

Of course, I'm the only one missing a doorman. My guy's probably still at attention on floor Chili Beef Soup waiting for me to get back from the lobby, saying *yes sir, right away sir, as you wish sir*, and doing absolutely fucking nothing.

I think he licked my finger, by the way. Early this morning, I dropped a five dollar bill and the damn thing butterflew off to the door, slid right under. And because I was half asleep, I stuck my fingers under the door, reaching for it, trying to catch it like it was about to fall down a gutter or through two planks on a pier.

Then something licked me. Not sexually but experimentally. Like the tongue was tasting something. I shivered and abandoned the five. If I had been more awake, I likely would have been suspicious about the whole affair, maybe even opened the door. Best case, and this is the best case scenario, it was an animal. Animals have no business roaming a hotel.

"He intends to play 'Für Elise' on that thing," Ed White says. A few accordion noises fall out.

"Is that so?" Sonia Salazar asks.

"Yes, of course, madam. I've played it before. I'm classically trained on the piano," he says with the waxed tips of his mustache wiggling.

"Could you handle the 'Turkish March'?" Sonia perks up. The cigarette holder has appeared. *I must have missed it,*

24

damn. For her, it's a speaking accessory. She points it and waves it like a conductor, demanding, no, controlling the expressions of everyone, everything, around her, maybe even the words themselves. This is her world, she is the choreographer. We're all dancers.

"I could handle any number, madam."

"Oh, I'd love to hear Bach. How about Bach?"

"Mr. Delivan has arranged for 'Für Elise.'"

Oh, I should tell you about the peacock. There's a trained peacock playing the centerpiece. He's standing frozen as a statue surrounded by a fruit arrangement, fighting every instinct not to peck at the fruits. He is not in his natural state. I want to describe him more, but that feels unnecessary. He's a peacock. A colorful male peacock like all the ones you've seen or heard about before. But let me stress again, he's standing as frozen as a statue, pretending to be a centerpiece. Imagine the money they spent on that training. And I don't even have a bathroom.

"Isn't it lovely?" Ms. Salazar says, catching my eyes watching the peacock. "He's just gorgeous."

Jesus, I'm still standing here like an idiot.

Eduardo Ruiz tells another dirty joke to Ed White who is too interested in Sonia Salazar's plate of cold cuts to hear it. She's got olive loaf, hard salami, serrano, and maybe chorizo. I'm not sure about the last one. Eduardo and Ed are both in freshly starched evening wear, red bow ties. They're fidgeting around, pulling at the collars, tugging at their pant seams, adjusting their cummerbunds, sweating

25

obviously. But they'd considered the sweating. A crisp bottled linen scent forms an olfactory shell around Ed White. For Eduardo Ruiz it's Arabian musk oil.

"Beautiful animals. You know, my father used to keep some," Ed says. "I've never seen a trained one. Fighting cocks. He kept those too. Those were—"

"What a bright blue." Sonia Salazar moves the charcuterie around her plate with a toothpick, not looking. The olive loaf captivates Ed. "Oh," she smiles. "So glad you're here finally, by the way," she says to me. "They're boring me to death with their dull jokes. Tell me something interesting." I hear *stop standing there, you're being weird*.

"I don't think we've met before, Ms. Salazar," I say.

"I know that, darling. But I asked for something interesting."

"Does your suite have a bathroom?" I ask.

"A bathroom? I should hope we don't need the bathroom for this conversation."

"No, it's—"

"Is there something you're needing to show me? I'll say it now, darling, I've seen it all before. No bathroom needed."

"No."

"I'll play along for a second, darling. Just a second. Yes, it does have a bathroom. A jacuzzi even. Mr. Delivan has outdone himself this go around, no doubt. Well, that wasn't interesting. A bathroom is quite ordinary. You know, I still do not like where this is going. Not at all."

26

"Sorry, it's… I, Mine doesn't have a bathroom. That's all."

"Here's another joke. A tall man and a sh—"

"Eduardo, I've had it up to here with your dull jokes." She turns to her doorman. "Excuse me, I'll have a mimosa." He doesn't respond. He stands as frozen as the peacock. "Excuse me? A mimosa, but make it with blood orange. I could not insult this beautiful creature. A bright juice will be such a breathtaking compliment to that blue, don't you think, darlings?" The doorman is still. "What is this? Excuse me. A mimosa."

"I'll get it," I say. "I was about to get one for myself." The peacock glances at me, moving his stone eye in a quiet twitch that only I can see. To everyone else he looks like a statue, and then he winks at me, unnoticed.

I can see the lust in his eyes, the hunger, the roaring desire to peck at the fruit, the cold cuts, at anything on that table, but he's stuck, frozen by employment, contractual obligation, domestic servitude, the constraints of social obligation. It would be uncouth to break form, and he's a highly skilled peacock.

"He was trained by lion tamers," the man with the accordion says, as if reading my thoughts. "He can forgo temptation, lust, better than any man." He pumps out the first few notes of "Für Elise" with a deep bow and a gliding backward step. It sounds like a piano with an orchestral backing.

"How does he do that?"

27

"Shh, quiet, darling. I want to listen."

I climb six steps to the refreshments table where there are three juice fountains, opened bottles of champagne, and a display of cocktail shrimp. Standing there, I can see the gray ocean again, over the stone masonry wall, and there it is: the banana bobbing up and down way off in the distance with the gulls gliding above it like vultures in that bizarre figure eight pattern. The peacock's eye catches mine again. He knows what I'm thinking; he's thinking the same thing, but he knows something I don't, about the banana, the loaf, the banana bread, the birds. Maybe about everything. Even life itself. A dog doesn't know what he doesn't know, and we're much the same way. We assume the peacock doesn't know what he doesn't know and especially doesn't know what we know he doesn't know, but in truth we don't know what he really knows or doesn't.

"Did you want mandarin? The blood orange looks off," I ask.

"Actually, mandarin sounds nice. Just a splash. A whisper even," she says.

"Maybe I should think of the first person to juice an orange while I fill the glass?"

"No, darling. Don't be dramatic." She grins.

I fill a glass with champagne. The juice is mostly frozen and a splash is really all that comes out of the spigot. It occurs to me, suddenly, that I'm still thirsty. The lobby water didn't do a thing for me. I take a milk glass to fill with juice, but nothing comes out from any spigot. I'll have to wait for the melt.

"How kind, darling." Sonia winks. "No bathroom. How utterly strange. I assume you're expected to use the one in the lobby, the one the peasants use?"

"They're migrants," Ed says. "Seasonal laborers. It's all above board, totally legal. Don't worry. There's a disclaimer at the back of your check-in packet."

"Why a disclaimer if it's all above board?"

"You know people. There's always so many questions."

"Ah, yes. I do that professionally, darling." She drops slightly, her shoulders lowering. "That lobby bathroom, my goodness, you poor thing. With that hideous *lumber* key chain like a roadside gas station." She turns towards me and crosses her legs.

I can't stand it. These little gestures, the tiny smile, those subtle movements that ignite. That weird "peasants" comment was sort of fucked up, but I can ignore that for now.

The peacock winks at me again. He knows what I'm thinking, feeling. His suffering is my suffering, though his lust is directed towards that food.

"I will say, darling, my room is lacking one amenity as well. I can't help but note your robe, quite cozy in fact. My closet is completely empty. Certainly, I'm just fine in my own skin. A little sun is good for the body, and the mosquitos never bother me. I've always felt just fine in my own skin."

"Maybe they're splitting up resources. Budgeting, the drought and whatnot. Did any of you get a glow-parrot? I saw a cage of them in the lobby."

"Yes, Ed, maybe so, darling. I can't say which I would prefer, the robe or a bathroom. Did those slippers come with the robe?"

"They did."

"All sorts of colors. Red, green, blue. A yellow one."

"A woman does need her make-ready time. I guess I can content myself with the bathroom and suffer the lack of spa attire. Do I look alright, darling?"

"Yes, yes of course. Your style is… avant garde."

"Natural, darling. I was going for natural."

"Tribal?" Ed asks.

"No, darling. I don't have the blood for that. Just natural, that's all. Natural."

'Tribal'? What's wrong with these people?

"So my invention is this." Eduardo Ruiz puts a black case on the table.

"Really, we should wait for Mr. Delivan before any business is discussed," Ed says.

"My god, business? I understood this to be relaxation. Why must you insist on being so dull so early?"

"He's ambitious, that's all," Ed says. "For him, business is relaxation. What's the point in inventing if you don't sell it?"

"It's a great idea. I'm excited to share it." He taps the case. "A part of me feels that the sooner the secret is out, the safer I am."

"You're not in any danger, darling. Trust me. No one

cares about the damn thing."

"I must insist that we wait for Mr. Delivan, or else you'll be doing your entire presentation all over again."

"I can only bear to hear it once, darling. I can't for the life of me figure out why the magazine is interested in this project at all."

"We really should wait," Ed says. "Mr. Delivan might take offense to your starting without him." He turns to me. "Hey, how about one of those mimosas?"

"Sure," I say. "I'm still up." I make his cocktail the same as I made Sonia Salazar's, then I try again for my own glass, but the juice is still too frozen for any more. I take my seat, and it's directly across from Sonia. *Pudge, you son of a bitch. Maybe you're not so bad.*

"Cheers, darling," she says, raising her flute.

"Cheers."

Someone serves me a black coffee in an art deco mug. It's garnished with a cinnamon stick. "What's this?" I ask.

"It's Mexican style, darling. Enjoy it. I asked for a latte, but, you know Mr. Delivan, he wanted something Mexican for Eduardo."

"Eduardo, you're Mexican?"

"No, I'm from Queens," he says. "I'm allergic to cinnamon." He shrugs.

"I asked for a latte," she says again.

"Could we get two lattes, please?" The waiter stares at me like he doesn't understand. "We don't want this." I try to give him my mug. He ignores me, standing at attention.

31

"Jesus." I take out the cinnamon stick, drop it on the bread plate. The coffee is cold, reeks of cinnamon.

"Just drink it, darling, don't be dull. We're guests here. If they can't bring a latte, we'll survive somehow."

"Will we though?"

"Ladies and gentlemen." Pudge marches into the Smoker's Garden through the elaborate double doors. "Breakfast is served." The doormen each march three steps backward and away, then ceremoniously return, simultaneously setting bowls of congee with prawns in front of us. "I'm afraid Mr. Delivan will not be joining this morning. Bon appetit."

"Is everything alright?" Ed asks.

"Quite alright, sir. Mr. Delivan insists that you enjoy your breakfast."

A naked gull says "squawk" at the edge of my hearing. I hadn't realized he was there.

The Woman

She lays in bed not sleeping or she sits on her folded legs at the open window's ledge smoking cigarettes, inhaling deeply and pursing her lips to puff into the open air. Her breath is an incense to the city that scrambles, scurries, beneath her. There's a bus still running. There are silhouettes at the bus stop, some with bags, some standing, others sitting, all looking tired. The glare of headlights beams from everywhere.

When she's in bed, it's white sheets, white pillows, a rotating ceiling fan, gardenias in a glass pitcher half filled with reverse osmosis water, shadows, books resting open upon their faces to mark their pages. Her hair is black, her eyes amber, sometimes honey, her skin is the same tone as his mother's (though he never knew that).

He imagines her flawless. He can't see the dried, crack-

33

ing skin on the tops of her hands that she moisturizes obsessively, treats with hydrocortisone, aloe vera clippings, avocado creams, magic crystals. He doesn't notice how her left eye opens wider than her right nor how her teeth are yellowed to several years above her age from coffee, cigarettes, red wine.

She lays on her side, under a sheet, with a pillow tucked between her knees and her feet poking outside of the sheet. She can't sleep, so she turns, picks up another book, drops it back down.

When she does sleep, she snores and drools. Her pillow at home is covered in stains. She turns again, and you can see the curves of her hips. She is a shadow backlit by the city.

She is wearing black cotton panties and a worn out tee because she is comfortable, but also because she is expecting a knock at the door, or maybe because she knows that that is what we imagine she would wear alone in bed.

She smokes at the open window, sitting on her bent legs, resting her neck against the sill, looking unusually comfortable, smirking even. Her skin reddens around the portion of her neck that touches the sill. There's a wrinkle forming at the crease of each eye, it touches her skin like the stroke of a charcoal artist. There's a tiny birthmark at the crest of her cheekbone, another at the crest of her lip on the same side of her face.

She exhales into the city, and the smoke spirals upward, refracting city light into the primary colors it hides in its white. She can't see the light or the colors because she's looking at her knee, running her fingers from the hand that doesn't hold the cigarette over her skin and thinking about her lavender body lotion. It works better than the last one.

She looks at the door, the city lights, the smoke, her own physical body, feeling in it *her warmth, her texture, her aches pains rambling thoughts itching with her lungs on each inhale first warmed up then satisfied then cooled with a breath outwards to be forgotten in infinite space where all things breathe or don't breathe and everything is eventually left behind.*

Everything is quiet, but everything exists in its own pattern and purpose or no purpose and moves in a direction towards or away from something, yet nothing, still, is happening. There is not a knock, a call, a note. There is not the shadow wandering the street to the building, not looking for her room, not looking for her door, not asking of her, not thinking of her. *There is just is, and it is now.*

3.

Eduardo Ruiz squirms in his chair. He hasn't touched the congee, but he's garnished it with dried mini shrimp, scallions, Chinese sausage, fish sauce, sesame oil, peanuts, and cilantro. We watch him drizzle or sprinkle basically all the toppings on top (proportions all fucked up) in the mindless, reckless, dangerous, blank-stared trance of a man about to jump from a building.

"My God, Eduardo. I hope you know what you're doing."

He taps one finger at a time on the top of the black case. It's squeezed between his shins and inward-pointing feet. He turns his head over his shoulder on either side, looking at the wall separating us from the ocean, the loaf of bread, the gulls, and the naked gulls.

"Maybe he's taken a lover, darlings. That sort of thing

37

can get one all tied up." Sonia shakes sugar off of a spoon into her coffee. "What a scandal. Could be my first gossip piece."

"Your first gossip piece was that bit on the President's… Russian fetish," I say.

"That was *not* gossip, darling. My sources checked out in every way."

"It was a strange one, I'll give him that, love," Ed says.

"Don't call me love, darling."

"I came all the way from Queens." Eduardo's knees bounce. His eyes wander, search, roll around in his head like in an 80's music video. "I don't think it's—"

"Take it easy, Eduardo. Tell another joke. Everything is fine. Mr. Delivan, he's… there's nothing to worry about." Ed White reaches to Eduardo's knee, but Eduardo slides his chair back from the table. "Really, it's fine," Ed tries to reassure him.

The dried shrimp start to soak up the liquid, stinking up the whole table.

"You put in too many dried shrimp, man," I say. "Scoop some out."

"You're not going to run away, are you darling?" Sonia stirs the coffee slowly, so slow that I wonder if it's mixing at all. The spoon scrapes against the walls of the mug and sounds like metal being dragged on a tile floor. "Surely, you're not worried. Mr. Delivan, I'm told he's… tell him." She looks at me.

"That's too much shrimp. It's going to taste awful."

"Tell him 'don't worry.'"

"Tell him what?"

"Tell him not to worry, darling. We're all here for the same reasons."

"I don't know about any of this." I stand up. "Is there a bathroom nearby?" The shrimp smell is nauseating.

 I'm losing it.

I can't stand being around this woman in this condition. What sort of torture is this? And devised by whom? If I'm in purgatory, send me one way or the other. I'm about done with this mess.

Here I'm exposed in the open amongst everything and everyone competing for the same attentions, esteems, affections, and my eyes are stuck, trapped, glued, fixed, fastened, welded, anchored, possessed by the woman sitting there, just there, and while everything pulls me towards her, all my animal instinct—desire, I'm aware—I can't see that I'm just another fat, slow wildebeest and those ripples, those flutters, that's a goddamned crocodile.

"Waiter." Eduardo Ruiz rises too, now clutching the case to his chest. "Call me a car, please. Immediately." The tall man halts his accordion playing and, with a head gesture, nudges the doorman standing behind Eduardo to go run off somewhere.

"Please sit down, gentlemen," the tall man orders. There is a locking sound from the double doors. Eduardo Ruiz obliges, and the man starts pumping his accordion again. I remember I'm standing, and I oblige too.

"You haven't touched your congee, darling. It's quite delicious. If I didn't know better, I'd say they flew it in this morning right from China. At least eat the prawns."

"How can he eat the prawns? They're covered in dried shrimp. He ruined them. Goddammit he ruined them."

"I came all the way from Queens for this."

"Relax. Here, have a cigarette." She snaps twice above her shoulder. One of the waiters, one that I haven't seen before, brings a silver tray with an entire silver cigarette setup: dispenser box, soft-flame fluid lighter and extinguisher cap, ashtray.

Sonia pulls out two cigarettes, loads one into her holder. The server takes the lighter, rolls the wheel, and holds the flame for her in what had to have been a meticulously rehearsed Lighting of the Tobacco ceremony.

"It's not too early, darling. You boys don't mind, do you," she says without the question in her voice.

She puffs.

The server sets the ignited lighter on the tray, extinguishes it with the extinguisher cap. I thought about blowing it out myself while he fussed with the tools, but I didn't.

"What happened with my stogie?" Ed White reaches across the table to grab a cigarette.

"Just say 'cigar,' darling. 'Stogie' is obnoxious. You sound like 90s Arnold."

"Sir, would you like to wait in your place? Until I'm ready to present the tray to you?" The waiter has a Make-

Way-for-the-Queen's-Guard! look in his eye.

"Can I at least get a whiskey? I mean, if we're smoking." Ed drops back into his chair.

"I ordered a cigar as well," I say. "...and a latte, if it's possible."

"Momentarily, gentlemen."

The double doors fly open again, and Pudge marches back in, grinning with his face pointing towards the sky like he might start singing. "A message for you, sir," he says to Eduardo. He bows, then he flips a folded square of paper from behind the palm of his white gloves, like performing a card trick.

Eduardo Ruiz reads the note before returning it to Pudge, who marches off with another bow. Eduardo leans over his congee, staring into it like it might tell him something about his fortune. His face calms as he sets the case back down on the ground between his legs. His knees continue to bounce.

"Mm," he says, taking in a heaping spoonful of congee. "Christ, this is terrible. How you guys eating this?"

"Well, I guess all is well? Not counting the congee." Sonia relaxes. Her bare chest is exposed from under the greenery.

"Mmhm. Says he'll make it for dessert."

Her cigarette points to the moon, which hasn't set yet, though the sun is lighting everything. Some of the gulls move closer. The naked ones start to hobble or swim over to congregate on the stone wall at the edge of the garden,

41

while the feathered ones circle overhead in that lopsided figure eight pattern. The two types really don't seem to fraternize. Life is not fair. It's never been fair as far as I can tell, and there sure are a lot of reminders. There are maybe seven or eight naked ones on the wall. They look miserable, sunburned. They're watching the peacock while the peacock watches me, Sonia Salazar watches Eduardo Ruiz, Ed White watches Sonia's olive loaf, and Eduardo Ruiz stares lost into his bowl of congee.

"Boy, your friend sure got all worked up, didn't he?" A naked gull says at the edge of my hearing.

"I guess so," I say.

4.

"Have a nice day, ladies and gentlemen." The peacock flutters his feet then makes his révérence. "It's been a pleasure." I rub my eyes with my palms, clean out each ear with the tips of my index fingers.

"Thank you, you were absolutely delightful," Sonia Salazar says, rolling her face towards me with a quick, hard glance.

The peacock bows again, hops off the table, and lands as gracefully as he stood. Then he goes to socialize with the gulls.

One of the naked gulls has harvested a cigarette butt and is smoking on top of the wall while the others loiter around him, saying "squawk." The peacock displays his feathers and eyespots while standing on one leg, shaking, then bouncing to the other. Squealer from *Animal Farm* comes to mind, but this peacock's got nothing to say.

"Join us if ya want," one of the naked gulls says, clicking a Bic lighter with his feet. *Jesus*, I think. *When did they start smoking?*

"Much obliged." The peacock glides to the wall, glancing at us with tightened eyes.

I can't take it anymore, so I climb the stairs to the refreshments table. The juices are still frozen. So are the cocktail shrimp. The presentation, the service, it all must be a joke. This is Mr. Delivan's secret revenge for who knows what. Or he thinks it's charming, some sort of a throwback to a different time when the idea of having frozen juice at all was a novelty.

The ocean is losing its gray to the rising sun, now favoring that bright green, but there it is: the banana loaf bobbing up and down. It's an island, and I think it's growing.

Or maybe I'm shrinking, maybe all of this is shrinking. Maybe this is the first step towards fading away into nothingness. Everything shrinks so that eventually, and sooner rather than later… we disappear.

I need to go. My mouth is dry. I might scream. All the juice is frozen, and I'm staring into an ocean that looks increasingly like green punch. But the salt is so dense you can taste it in the air.

"Ms. Salazar," I say. "Are you going to finish your drink?" *Yes, I'm that desperate*, I preemptively respond in my head.

"My goodness. No, darling, by all means." She slides

the glass to my place on the table as I nearly run down the steps. "I'm switching to whiskey. The sun's up. And it's Sonia, please. We're all friends here. Especially if we're sharing glasses now. Are you really that thirsty?"

"The juice is frozen, look. Even the cocktail shrimp are frozen. Squeeze one of them… and I'm—that's about all I can take, asking for water. I don't. I—This place is a desert."

"Dessert?" Ed White's interest is piqued.

"Desert," I say.

"Just drink, darling, no one cares. You're getting all worked up."

Her champagne burns my throat. Three swallows and it's gone. It's room temperature, and, though it's an extra brut, the sugar makes me feel even more thirsty.

I catch myself staring at the damn frozen juice. The conversation in front of me is a blur. Sonia's laugh, her smile, her quips about whatever it is that's making Ed White nervous and Eduardo Ruiz anxious—I can't hear them.

It's hypnosis, the drops of juice building up and falling from the ice chunks, the roar of the ocean, the salt in the air, the sun somehow biting through the clouds, the peacock dancing for naked gulls.

I won't stay here. I'll check out today, go home, sleep. Drink some fresh water, go to my own bathroom, or any bathroom.

"I'll have whiskey, too. And a glass of water, please. Seriously, water," I say.

"Right away, sir."

He comes back with just the whiskey.

I'm so thirsty, I scoop out the ice cube (it's one of those giant spheres from Mr. Delivan's specialist), I crack it on the table and eat it, sucking on each fragment, but in the end I'm still thirsty. I can feel those tiny sugar bumps growing on the back of my throat. Do you ever get those? This is outrageous.

"Water must be precious here," I say.

"Water is precious everywhere, darling." Sonia watches the naked gulls. I wonder if she's also wondering when they took up cigarettes. Their numbers are growing. Maybe fifteen of them now sit on or around the stone wall, silent, their beaks somehow frowning. The peacock is still fanning his feathers, putting on a little dance for them, and they're all looking, no, glaring, at us.

We did nothing wrong, I want to say. *We're just guests here, you know. Mr. Delivan invited, insisted, that we come.*

"No, Ed. Don't feed them, darling. They'll gather around."

"Please, don't feed the gulls, sir. Hotel policy. My apologies. If you'd like, we do accept donations for a local rescue organization."

"It's just a chunk of bread."

"All the same, sir. The hotel must insist that guests do not feed the gulls."

"So tell me," Sonia says. "Have you been here before? I understand this hotel was designed by Andy Warhol. Can you imagine that?"

"I heard the same."

"It's nothing like his art. At least none that I've seen. Except for that dreadful elevator with the obnoxious buttons. I must have pressed six options to find the Smoker's Garden. And by the way, is there a Non-Smoker's Garden? How dull that must be."

"There is, Madam, one floor above."

"The terrace just there?" She cranks her neck.

"You can't see them, Madam. There are screens to guard them from the sun."

"Dull, indeed. Darling, would it be impolite to ask that you leave the bottle on the table? I've spent quite a bit of time in Central America, and the most posh restaurants, they'll just leave the bottle right there on the table for us. You can mark it if you'd like. Charge us when you see what's left."

"I think that would be fine." He checks the expressions of the other servers, the doormen. No one seems to object. "Well, here it is. Now it's a party, I should say, madam." He notches the bottle with a black wax marker.

"Very good, darling." She pinches his cheek.

"I don't understand that. I never have," Ed White says, finally getting his first cigarette.

"What's that, darling?"

"A Non-Smoker's Garden. We're all outside here. Indoors, sure. A restaurant or some place like that, I understand. But why a separate outdoor garden?"

"Well, it's simple, darling. The Non-Smokers could fall

47

over dead at the sight of us. It's all a hotel liability problem. God knows the aroma, excuse me, the stench alone is so noxious that one whiff sends them into a coughing fit. Excuse me one second," she pauses for an exaggerated inhale and exhales rings of smoke. "They're like little bunnies, darling, little bunnies who've seen a wolf. Their hearts stop right then and there, and they fall over dead. Why do you think they have the screens? They can't see the sun either, just as dangerous."

"I bet they have juice up there, not frozen. Maybe I'll run up there and check."

"No juice, sir. Only Diet Coke," a doorman says.

"That's all they have up there?"

"And turkey burgers, sir. Besides, I'm afraid the hotel must insist that you enjoy the Smoker's Garden due to your classification."

The double doors pop open, sending some of the gulls fluttering their wings while not taking flight, and Pudge, the fat son of a bitch, delivers another note to Eduardo Ruiz.

"Well." Eduardo stands, shoving the note into his pants pocket. "I hope this hasn't been a wasted trip for all of us. Looks like we are completely delayed until tomorrow morning."

"What?" Ed White shakes his head. "Nothing for me?"

"No, sir."

"The note just says: 'Same time tomorrow. Apologies. -Del.'"

"That's no reason we can't enjoy a little sun and re-

48

freshments, darlings. Sir, how about mojitos? Can you do mojitos here? Do you boys like mojitos? All the rage in el Ca-rib."

"El Caribe," I say. "The i is like ee, and the e is like eh."

"Of course, madam, right away."

"Naturally, darling. That's what I said, more or less."

"I think I'll go back up to my room. Try to sleep for a bit. I couldn't get any sleep last night," I say.

"At least finish your whiskey, darling. They went all the way to the kitchen to get it."

"I heard they offer a boat tour. There was a flier in the lobby. Could be a time," Ed White says.

"Entirely too much work."

"It's a nice day at least."

"There's nothing but clouds, darling. It's dreadful for an oceanside day."

"If you'll excuse me," I say. "I'll see you at dinner."

"Dinner it is," Ed says.

Eduardo Ruiz stops, hunched over with a spoonful of congee at the edge of his mouth. "What floor are you on?"

"Turkey Noodle, I think? This whole system drives me nuts."

"Enjoy your nap, darling."

"Oh Christ, don't tell me you're doing the boat tour," a naked gull says to me. "We're going to have to scrub the whole damn island."

5.

The bathroom in the lobby looks like it might be empty. The lights are off, and the candle outside the door is on its last breath. A drooping leaf from a house plant covers the unisex wall sign so that it's all legs.

I decide to sneak a visit before heading up, but the door's locked. I do the tug, shake, jiggle one does. I can't deal with Pudge. I'm about to walk away or kick the damn thing or ram it or steal the key or run right out the door and pee over the stone wall into the ocean, but someone opens the door. *Goddammit, it's Pudge.*

"It's the way she looks at you. I know, cliché, but cliché… there's truth in it, otherwise it would've never made it to cliché status." Pudge walks backward, pulling me in with a frankly seductive hand motion.

"You need to calm down," I say.

51

"You calm down." He sits on the trunk of the elephant chair, and struggles with a matchbox and a colonial clay pipe. "Yeah, that was weird. Sorry. I was going for secretive."

"On break again?"

"It's a Union gig."

"I thought you were a volunteer," I say. "I don't even know what to say about you tying up the bathroom like it's your own private lounge."

"It is private." He shrugs. "I don't get a lot of privacy around here. I'm sort of the main man when Mr. Delivan is busy. Besides, we don't have a break room. Where else would I go?"

"The garden, your office, a seaside terrace, a room no one is using."

"We have rules here."

"Do you?" There's a basket of toothbrushes rolled up in paper napkins next to a pump bottle of toothpaste. I don't ask, just start brushing. The flavor is awful, like baking soda and wilted spearmint. I can almost feel it eating away at my enamel, pinging in the grooves and divots of my teeth like battery shocks.

"It's the way she looks at you, I was saying." He gets a match going. The first few puffs smell like incense, churchy-sweet and serious.

"How do you mean?" I spit toothpaste into the sink, turn on the water.

"Exactly how I said. It's the way she looks at you. It was

that moment in the Smoker's Garden. She was stirring her coffee with her cinnamon stick. There was something in her eyes. Mr. Delivan saw it too."

"Mr. Delivan?"

"He was behind me. He saw her eyes. He saw the way she looked at you. The best part, you didn't even notice."

"There's nothing in me, not for—"

"Yeah, yeah, not for her. She's out of your league, etc. We get it."

"You're just fucking with me. Because of the whole bathroom situation."

"Fucking with you is when you get the minibar charge for that toothbrush."

"That toothpaste is rancid, by the way."

"It's hand soap."

"Spearmint hand soap?"

"What's wrong with that?"

"Why would you put it next to the toothbrush basket?"

"I didn't put it anywhere. Listen, I'm serious. That's why he sent the note to Mr. Ruiz, why he canceled the meeting."

"She doesn't even know my name."

"She doesn't have to know your name. What's in a name, right? Bill said that." He sparks another match. "How do you get this thing going?"

"Listen," I put my hand on his shoulder. "I'm about done with all this. Can you call me a car? I'm going back to the city. No offense. Unless you can find me a room with a sink and a toilet. Maybe some toothpaste, a bottle of water. Some guest services."

"You can stay in this room."

"I don't want just a bathroom. I want a complete room. A standard hotel room."

"The fact that your room is in the hotel makes it a standard hotel room."

"I disagree. Can you move me to a complete room?"

"'Complete' is relative. Plus, I'm afraid we are booked solid. Have you ever used one of these clay pipes?"

"Alright. Call me a car please. I'll be down in twenty minutes."

"You'll need to see reception to check out."

"You are reception."

"I'm on a break."

"Okay. When will you be back?"

"Twenty minutes."

"Great. I'll be down in twenty minutes."

"So, anyway. I was saying. Her eyes, did you notice how she was looking at you?"

"Are we back to that again?"

"Why not? There's not much to talk about here."

"So what's your theory then? Can I at least use the commode while you ramble?"

"I'd have to check the roster, but I'm on break. Besides, it's occupied."

"Jesus."

"There's a look that women get, actually, no, I take that

54

back. There's a look that all people get. It's buried deep in their eyes, past the little black part."

"The pupils?"

"Yes, past that. Behind it really. Behind the pupils, there are tiny mirrors."

"Mirrors." I feel the door behind me reaching out. I may turn and run.

"Yes, basic glass mirrors. They're right behind the pupils, on everyone. Even people who can't see. Everyone except the dead. In these mirrors, it's possible, if you know how to look for it, to see a flash of light. Look close at people next time you're walking around, or whatever you do, look at their eyes. Look close. If you learn how to do it, you can see the flash. But, here's the thing, the flash doesn't show for everyone. It's there though, under the right conditions."

"I'll be down in twenty to check out."

"Sure." He shrugs. "Looking forward to it."

"Weren't there two sinks here?" I ask.

"How should I know?"

"Forget it."

The Woman

She'll watch it spin all night if she has to she'll watch the damn thing spin and spin and everything else that goes with it what is it except the world it's all spinning anyway or maybe it's us that are spinning and everything else is quiet still and waiting for the next role or the next life or the next calling the first calling even the one we all missed that told us we were supposed to be natural animals living in our own skin eating wild fruits and nuts and chasing meat to eat raw only focused on survival only focused on being alive and living without ever thinking about why or how or when or where just here here now here we are here we've always been as far as we were told and maybe that way we would have never been told anything other than don't stay too long at the river there's crocodiles in there they'll eat you like you eat the meat we chase...

She stops. Can you see her? She's hurting there on the floor with the blankets cast aside and the candle flickering from the open-window breeze.

Here I am do you see me do you see me goddammit I exist I exist just like you I hurt and love and feel and cry just like you do you see me or not

The wind wants to blow. She wants to touch her, guide her, lift her, take her somewhere where wild grass grows green with golden panicles under natural sun unhampered by human corruption, where there's clean water to drink, but she can't; the window is only cracked, and it's jammed with the same city sounds that clog her ears.

The ears to whom she, the wind, would say: *you're alright. Everything is alright, follow me here.* Transparent hands touch the glass, drift away, and disappear into space and time, and she looks out the window not seeing the wind, feeling her, smelling the scents of life carried up from the street, touching the moisture of recent rain in her breath, and that's it. This is her existing.

6.

Sticks, with Pudge watching over his shoulder, sorts through a stack of papers about a hundred sheets deep. He pounds the bottom of each page with a rotary stamp. Another guest, someone I haven't seen before, is waiting on the red velvet sofa. Mr. Peacock is performing a yoga-esque pose on the reception desk, standing next to the brass bell.

"Good morning, sir," Pudge says.

"Checking out." I roll my eyes, shake my head. "My doorman said you'd call my room to bring my bags down."

"That's right. The guest attendant manager is preparing your checkout application."

"Application? Guest attendant manager? You mean Sticks?"

"Yes. Who? No. Yes."

"I don't need an application. I'm going to give you my

59

room key, you're going to call me a car, and that's it."

"Certainly, sir."

"Alright, so take the key." He looks at it on the counter where I've dropped it.

"I'm afraid, you see, sir, because Mr. Delivan is covering all the expenses, you are in fact required to fill out the checkout application."

"Why is that?"

"Any changes to the itinerary need to be approved by Mr. Delivan personally."

"That's an easy fix. Let's call his room."

"He's indisposed."

"I've never filled out an application to check out of a hotel. I can't remember a time where I ever filled out any paperwork at all."

"It's a customs and immigration problem."

"I thought it was a Mr. Delivan issue."

"Not exactly. Because Mr. Delivan has arranged every-thing, and all the paperwork has been submitted to the au-thorities with his specific itinerary, any changes, including your premature departure, must be approved by Mr. Deli-van and, as you can imagine, the proper authorities, before I can legally call you a car."

"You're kidding."

"I am not."

"Alright, give me the sheet. I'll fill it out." I click the pen laying on the desk.

"It's not ready yet, sir. The guest attendant manager is

preparing it now."

"You mean Sticks?"

"The guest attendant manager, sir."

"That stack there?"

"Yes, sir."

"How many people are checking out?"

"Just you, sir."

"That's a hundred pages."

"One hundred twenty-seven." He grins with feigned re-assurance. The sort of grin I'd imagine I'd see if mortally wounded and asking, "Am I alright? Is it bad?" *No, not bad at all. You look great, buddy. You're going to be just fine.*

"I'm in a Kafka story. This is a nightmare." I clench the pen. I think about throwing it across the lobby towards the door, but that sort of behavior won't help this situation. Besides, this could just be another twisted art joke.

"Rest assured, sir, you are not," he says.

"His photo is right there on the wall!" No joke, hanging on the wall behind the desk is a picture of Franz Kafka standing next to Andy Warhol in front of a painting of a bonsai.

"No, sir. That's Mr. Delivan."

"This is a joke, another twisted art joke."

"It is not." The grin falls away to reveal something more serious, his lips now a flat line.

I've never actually seen Mr. Delivan. Through all of our business, all of our correspondence, I've never met the man. Ed White always handled the person-to-person stuff.

"That's Mr. Delivan?"

"From years ago, yes, sir."

"I've never actually met him. I… when will my packet be ready?"

"Tomorrow after breakfast." Sticks throws his voice over his shoulder.

"Tomorrow." Pudge clears his throat. "After breakfast. Can I offer you some pamphlets on guest activities? There is a birdwatching boat tour in an hour. The sign-up sheet is on that wall."

"Which room is Mr. Delivan in?"

"I'm afraid that's confidential."

"Can you phone his room, let him know I'd like to see him."

"I can have a runner send word."

"That's fine," I say.

"Go ahead, write what you want." He slides some stationary to me.

I jot down a few lines, fold it in half. "Here." I give it to Pudge.

I turn back to the waiting man. He's standing now. The sofa is gone. I think *Christ, I need to sleep.*

Naked Gulls

The sun is almost gone for the night, and the fat boy checks the window to make sure it's gone, or he checks his watch and compares the time to the sunset forecast in the newspaper's weather section, reading and re-reading at the edge of the empty lobby. It's so empty that he feels comfortable having left open the door to the office with a leg of his cot visible. He's content with the way headlights shine from well down the drive and provide him with sufficient warning of a potential guest's approach. The private cars only come at night, and he expects none tonight.

He checks again. The sun is definitely gone. With one of those deep, exhausted exhales conditioned by monotony, he goes to his office to pull on the yellow waders, the kind crab fishermen wear. He centers the desk bell and puts a small framed sign on a brass stand on the desk: "Will Return. 20 Minutes."

The service elevator takes him to floor Pepper Pot, opens with a ding. He is on the opposite side of the stone wall from the Smoker's Garden, overlooking a cove. There's a wooden boat there, tied to a wooden post, discreetly positioned so as not to be visible from any of the areas authorized for guest use. He tosses a bag with some snacks and a bottle of water into the boat, then he flips through the keys on a brass loop until he finds the one that unlocks the door to the bread closet.

It's a white, shabby door, maybe even professionally distressed, and it looks light, but it's heavy. It opens outward.

Inside is a deep, narrow room lit by office-style tube lighting. Along either wall are shelves stacked with wide loaves of an almost flat bread. At the end, at the back wall, there is a short, fat man baking the bread over oak coals in a clay oven. The smoke pipes out through a vent at the top of the hotel. He says nothing, just nods at the fat boy who nods back.

The fat boy clears his throat, then he notices he's still wearing his white uniform gloves. He sighs, shoves them into the inside pocket of the waders, and pulls on a pair of gardener's gloves that were hanging on a shovel's handle at the door frame. They have a floral pattern and green rubber accents.

The baker nods again, this time towards a plastic bag tied with a string, and the fat boy nods back, picking it up.

✳✳✳✳✳

The sea air is cold. He is rowing out towards a fog that hovers in a blur, hiding the horizon. At the clunking of his oars, gulls begin to circle over him. A chill touches his legs through the waders, and the ringing of a distant emergency vehicle siren makes him shudder. The water laps slowly, licking the sides of the boat. Tasting it, retreating.

He rows for fifteen minutes, his back turned to the island. Instead of looking behind himself for the discoloration at the edge of the bread island and the dune it sits on, he looks straight ahead, gauging his distance away from the island by tracking his proximity from the hotel, which now stands in the center right of his field of view.

From the picture before him, he knows he's almost there. It's a sloshy thump when the dinghy hits the dune. There's only one naked gull there, but he can see the others at the opposite edge.

"Hey," the gull says. "More bread?" The fat boy struggles out of the dinghy, carrying the bag over his shoulder. He looks like a peculiar Santa Claus. Feeling around in the water, he locates the string, then follows it back until he reaches the pulley, which he struggles to crank, but manages to get going. The string is lined with plastic trays pigmented the same gray as the ocean. As each plastic tray passes, he drops a loaf of bread on it then keeps cranking. He sends about twenty loaves.

He's done and leaving. The naked gulls are gathering

65

around, chatting quietly amongst themselves while the feathered gulls squawk in flight above. Rowing away, he smiles.

"Shit," he says, thrusting the oars flat into the water to stop. "I'm sorry. I'm coming back. I'll be right back. Let me turn around," he shouts.

"We thought you forgot."

"No. Well, almost. But, hold on." The dinghy lands with the same sloshing thump. He takes out a stick of incense from the inside of his waders, burns it with his eyes closed, mumbling something sort of like a prayer. "There. See you tomorrow," he says, and tosses the half-burned incense stick into the water. The breeze hides the hiss of its extinguishment.

7.

Pudge, dressed up like an Alaskan fisherman, is our tour guide. There's no mercy in this place. On the tour, it's me, Sonia Salazar, and a Norwegian woman from another group who keeps plugging her nose and asking "is someone smoking?" We've each been issued a set of binoculars, a headset, and a light-blue low-density polyurethane poncho-style rain cover.

Pudge, assisted by six or so others, is yanking a ratty dinghy from a shed towards the Smoker's Garden, where we're waiting. It's scraping through the mud, parting the clay much less biblically than the Red Sea was, but Pudge seems impressed with himself. It hits the water with a percussive whomp. He dives into the boat, pushing it out, turning it parallel to the beach. The helpers march back inside.

"Ladies and gentlemen, you are free to board from the

port side." We have to hop the stone wall to traverse a dozen yards of beach mud, wade through knee-deep water to reach the edge of the boat, then struggle in by flopping over the sides like tuna, all while Pudge stands there with his legs wide apart, pretending to sturdy the boat.

Inside: wooden planks painted blue, faded to gray, then painted blue again for what I would guess is all of time, and the occasional yellow board shining through like sun somewhere beyond the clouds. An old rope, coiled, frayed. Moldy life jackets, orange. Long, white wooden benches totalling four rows. Did I mention the interior wood is totally gray like an ash in winter? Lines of black cracks running through like veins. The smell of mold, salt, algae. You know, from the sea. It feels more like a Southeast Asian longboat than a dinghy.

Actually, it is a longboat. I guess I was being condescending with the dinghy comments. Or it's the vibe here skewing my perspective, or it's Pudge's general way of being and my resulting disdain for all things Pudge. I don't know. It's not a dinghy after all, that's what I mean to say. There's a small engine on the back.

"Why do we have to row?" I ask, and point to the engine.

"We advise that our guests enjoy a natural experience."

"But we can use the motor."

"No comments during the presentation, please."

For a split second, the ocean is not an ocean either, nor is the island an island. For that moment halfway through a blink, I see under my eyelids a field of wheat, and the island is a bale of hay, the gulls are crows, and the wind….well, it's still the wind, but dry and with a different voice. I can see it over the water now, like a double exposure.

Sonia floats away into the horizon, but her body sits in front of me. She's dressed for winter now even though it's warm, a distinct contrast to the fishermen's getup Pudge has on. "I'm worried about the breeze, darling." Her eyes are shocking. Deep and piercing, filled with words that she doesn't have to speak.

"A safe choice, madam," Pudge says.

Me and the Norwegian are dressed for Mexican beach summer, except we're missing the lagers and limes. My outfit was delivered by my doorman. I can't speak for the Norwegian. I feel heavy, tired. I could finally sleep if I could just lie back across the bench. There's just enough mix of sun, fresh air, tranquility to close my eyes, but our task is to row, row in sync towards that giant loaf of bread where the gulls and naked gulls gather.

Pudge drones on about the different forms of plant life at the edge of the sea, the nature of the gulls, theories on the origins of the naked gulls. Sonia is not rowing. It's just me and the Norwegian propelling the vessel, and it doesn't seem like we're moving at all.

She's lost somewhere, Sonia is, and it's far away, past where her eyes wander, past where they're trying to see. I want to touch her shoulder, but I know it would jolt her back, and I know that right now, in this moment, she needs

69

to be wherever she is, and I need to be here floating in an ocean, paddling but not moving, hearing only the sounds of plopping oars and the brushing breeze, filling my vision with endless gray water to a horizon mingling with gray clouds, touched at the base by an island of bread and gulls. If I were to paint this, the painting would be a canvas of layered, textured gray pigments. In the center, there would be a small square of pale, maybe translucent yellow, and on that square would be white dots and yellow dots, and above that square would be white dots in the empty gray.

"Is someone smoking?"

"No, lady. Again. No one is smoking," I say. "No one in this boat has smoked all day."

"Just a reminder, ladies and gentleman, smoking is strictly prohibited on this tour. Thank you."

We stop. Pudge leans forward off the bow, points ahead. "And there it is, ladies and gentlemen."

"It doesn't seem like we're much closer than we were," I say.

"We must maintain a respectful distance, so as not to disturb them."

"I do say, darling, I have to agree with my friend. The view is not much different from my balcony," Sonia says without turning her head away from that far-off place. We hear her voice but only see the back of her hood.

"You have a balcony?" I ask. She says nothing.

"Which one is it? That thing there?" The Norwegian asks.

"There. Right there. Do you see the gulls circling above?"

"Yes."

"Below that. The little mound. It looks like a banana."

"Oh, yes. And why are the gulls naked?"

"There are many theories, madam. This was covered in the presentation."

"I'm sorry to have missed it."

"She's quite right, darling. You were droning on, and quite dull about it."

"Would you tell me again?"

"I'm afraid the tour only covers one reading of the guide transcript."

"Basically," I say. "Some believe it's a skin disease, others a curse, some a genetic mutation, and yet others still, that they are in fact not gulls at all, but some other animal entirely."

"Hasn't anyone just asked the damned things?"

"Of course, madam. They respond either with silence or by saying 'here I am. I was here yesterday.'"

"I'd be surprised if they were something other than gulls. They sound just like the other birds. The ones with language, anyway. They look alike. Everything but the feathers."

"I agree," Pudge says. "Off the record."

"It seems the feathered ones frequently beg for fish," the Norwegian says.

"I can't say I recall a naked gull ever asking for fish."

71

"They eat the bread, madam."

"Ah, yes. Well that does imply a different animal, doesn't it? Or at least a different species?"

"Possibly," Pudge says. "But it could just be an evolutionary adaptation. No feathers means no flight, no flight means no fishing, no fishing means no food. So they eat bread."

"I see."

"Yes." He clears his throat. "That concludes the tour, ladies and gentleman. If everyone will dip their port-side oar, holding it straight in, and paddle on three with your starboard oar in three… two… one… paddle."

"They're not birds at all," I say. "Look at them." I stand up, the others grab the sides of the boat from the sudden unsteadiness. "What the hell are you?" I shout. "You're not birds."

"Here I am, squawk. Here I was yesterday."

"I told you," Pudge says.

"Oh, I say. I could do this story. Maybe Nat Geo would go for it, darling. It could be an entirely lovely change of pace for me. I could sport a safari getup for the photographs, even."

"You could," I say.

"But do I write it as an infestation? An invasion maybe? Or just a natural wonder? That's always the hard part of any story."

"Just write it as it is, right? You know, just the facts, ma'am."

"No, no, darling. Clearly, you've never written for an editor."

The Woman

In bed again, she's wide awake. The lights and shadows on her face are patterned like they're reflected from a disco ball, but their origin is unknown, and she doesn't seem to notice the way they touch her, collect on her skin like gathering water, evaporate and drop again, desire to carry her off, show her their source or feed her with the same in an enlightenment we can't understand.

She's watching the ceiling fan rotate or she's counting the moon dots on the wall opposite the open windows. Her hand rests on her stomach, adjusting in delicate motions when motion is necessary. Her ankles are crossed. She's painted her toenails, but their color is uncertain in the dimness.

The sheets drape over her thighs, and her head is on a pillow. We'd expect her to be cold with the way the breeze flaps the curtains, but she's neither cold nor hot, she's waiting. She wonders whether the coming light is the emerging of the sun or the city's nightlife, but she knows it's too late or too early to really be either.

An ashtray positioned where she thinks her hand would naturally fall if she fell asleep holds two crushed cigarette butts; a cocktail glass on the window sill holds three more; a dozen butts are scattered, one as far as a block away, on the street below.

She thinks about how she shouldn't smoke in bed, about how dangerous that is, about the article she read where the woman burned her house down, and she smirks, feeling reckless in a subtle, private recklessness that no one else knows about. If someone knocked at her door, she'd jump up, hide the ashtray, and toss the cigarette pack and lighter to the chair or desk.

On her desk, a stack of blank paper flutters under a black rock. A fountain pen drips black ink on the black wood. The desk chair is toppled over, or thrown over. Whatever happened, it's not standing nor has it been set upright. A fluff of lint hangs from the chair's wheel. If she's thought about going back to the desk, it hasn't shown. She rubs her ankles together to the same slow beat of the fan's rotation.

Another cigarette in her mouth, the cherry glowing, burning down like a cone of incense. The ceiling will open to the sky if she blinks fast enough or stares hard enough. She'll see through it beyond the lights, plaster, bricks, the clouds, satellites, through the universe. If she keeps her eyes wide open or closes them tight enough, she will see past it all. It will all make sense.

Orgy Floor

He did go to the orgy floor, but he'd never write about it past the mentioning that it exists, and the pages he did type went to the trash bin. The fat boy doormans the thing for cash tips and a hundred a night on a 1099 pay stub labeled "consulting" that he stores in his breast pocket in case of questioning. The uniform is different. Black suit, black tie, white shirt, like a Tarantino character.

"Would you like to rent a suit jacket, sir?" the fat boy asks.

"I, yes, okay."

"Allow me." He takes the robe, helps him into a suit jacket. "The tie is in the pocket."

"I'm wearing a t-shirt."

"Necktie required."

"This is, the… um."

"Indulgence Room."

"I, alright."

"Allow me, sir," the fat boy says. "Your hands are shaking."

"I didn't expect—"

"This floor is discreet, sir. There's nothing to worry about." He straightens the necktie. "There you are. And quite sharp, if I may say."

He stands at the double doors. They're churchy, stained mahogany, carved. The fat boy steps aside, points behind himself, then raises his arm in a backward salute, maybe a dab, that covers his eyes. He's only a minor and should not look inside.

First it's casino bells from slot machines to his left, then the humming of hidden overhead air filtration systems above. The ceilings are high. Everything is lit a dim yellow except for whatever it is that's to his right, where there are only movie-theater or airplane style emergency lights, shadows that seem like persons, and variations in the black that suggest smaller rooms, secret rooms, private corners.

And, *my god*. She's there. She's at a roulette table and they all circle around watching, feeling her exist next to them, feeling their own existence in her glow, and he thinks *fuck it I'm leaving*, but he doesn't leave.

They share a glance and a smile, someone offers a flute of champagne and he takes it, raises it, and she raises a double rocks glass of something neat. She winks but it's not an invitation, it's only a greeting so he wanders first through

80

aisles of slots then past game tables but he's drawn to the unlit.

Sound stops at the edge of the yellow light. There's only breath and the humming of the air purifiers, the HVAC, and the static of a single television with no signal whose screen has been stenciled over to display the words "Private Rooms" in the distortion.

"Your coat, sir?" a tuxedoed man asks.

"Yes, alright."

"A room, sir?"

"Oh, no. It's just me."

"They're all waiting for you in the room, sir."

He is silent.

"Right this way," the tuxedoed man says, holding the coat over his arm, spotting the label emblem that identifies it as hotel property and routes it to a closet separate from the guest-owned coats closet. "Follow me, please." And he does follow.

The room is quiet, dark, and small. There is a black recliner, some cords. He sits feeling nervous expectation and the desire to flee.

"Your headset, sir."

"Headset?"

"Yes, sir."

8.

I wake up with a dehydration headache to the pop of a gull crashing into the window. The sound bounces around my skull, hitting all the walls, echoing against the nerves. He's smacked it hard enough to leave blood and shatter the tempered glass, which didn't fall.

Is that beak blood? Maybe general head blood. There's no way the bird survived. The blood is smeared around in a circle as if someone tried to wipe it off with too little newspaper. He's gone, as is his body, fallen into the mud, sand, long green grass, or even the ocean water, but he's left a little note at the window's edge, rolled up quite formally into a scroll. It's got to be a suicide note. Jesus, I think. I reach for the phone, but it's off the hook and there's no dial tone.

Someone clears their throat, and I feel warmth, breath

against my neck moistened with the humidity of life. Sonia Salazar is pressed against me and as naked as I am. *What the fuck.* I want to speak, to shake her awake, to put my hands on her body and pull her closer to me, but I can't get a word out, and all of my muscles are frozen. Instead, I glide my arm out from under her. *Jesus, look at her.* I'll never understand it: how man has the capacity to feel all of this from the closed eyes of a sleeping woman.

I follow the phone cord to the wall and plug it back in. I click the hang up button a couple of times until the dial tone kicks in, then I call down to the front desk.

"There's been an incident," I whisper. "A bird—"

"A seagull, sir."

"Yes, a gull. A gull has flown—"

"A seagull has crashed into your window, killed itself, and left behind a note?"

"Uhm, yes. Yes, exactly."

"Huhhh," he sighs. "I'll send someone up shortly."

"Thank you."

Sonia stretches and sits up. "Ah, good morning, darling, what a bright sun." She pauses. "Was your window like that before?"

"No, a bird hit it."

"Feathered or naked?"

"Feathered, but he left a note."

"Strange. Is there coffee?" She climbs out of bed and stands in front of the window.

"No, sorry. This room doesn't have a coffee maker. We

84

could go down to the Smoker's Garden?" Her eyes look past, through the shattered tempered glass, out into the ocean. Her eyes catch mine on her body, and she pulls the sheet from the bed, wraps herself up. I grab my spa robe from the floor and struggle into it as quickly as I can.

"Don't make too much of it, darling. Last night was very, very cold," she says, spinning the sheet around her, moving to a window she can see through.

"When did you come in?"

"You gave me a key, did you forget?"

"Well, yes. I guess I did."

"At brunch, darling. You gave me a key. Don't tell me you weren't freezing to death last night. I practically saved your life. I know you saved mine. You're like a personal space heater. How did you sleep, darling?"

"I… fine, thank you. You?"

"Just great. Shall we head to the Smoker's Garden? I understand there's another breakfast too, not just coffee."

"Yeah, sure." I open the nightstand. There's not an aspirin in this place. "We, uhm, we'll have to go to the lobby to get ready."

"I'll swing by my own room, don't worry. I'll see you in the Garden." The door shuts behind her. *Don't go. Don't ever go, just stay here and let the world swim by, forgetting us, forgetting me, and we'll forget her too right here in the bed, watching the ocean, breathing the salt, knowing each other.*

My head.

I dig around a little more for a bottle of aspirin, but I

85

can't find anything. My spa slippers are still by the door. The doorman is rustling with something out there, so I pull the door open.

"Can I get some aspirins?"

"Right away, sir." He snaps his heels, salutes, but doesn't move.

"May I have them now, please?"

"Yes, sir." He snaps his heels again.

"Will you be going then?"

"Yes, sir. Right away, sir."

"It seems like you're not going."

"Correct, sir. We do not leave our post."

"How will you get my aspirins?"

"Right away, sir." He snaps, salutes.

"I see."

"Yes, sir."

"Alright." I don't bother to close the door, and I fall into the armchair facing the shattered-in-place window. The scroll is outside the window. I'm curious to read it. Maybe it contains instructions, advice, something that would be valuable to the authorities or his survivors, but maybe it's not my business. Maybe the authorities should be the ones to decide that.

"Knock knock."

"Yes?"

"We're here to fix the window." The two blue jumpsuits come in carrying plate glass with suction cups. They look like hitmen. A third comes in with a shop vac. "You'll have to wait in the lobby."

"I was just headed that way."

"The desk will notify you when it's done." The shop vac flips on, pulling in the window like a sheet of fabric. Ocean sun floods in. The sound and the light jolt me so much that I back out of the room with my eyes wincing and my fingers pressing into my temples.

"Thank you," I say.

Dragging my feet down the hallway, I lose the shop vac to find a maid's vacuum and the beat of music coming from an open door. She's in there dancing and driving the vacuum with swinging hips. *Lord baby Jesus on the cross, two aspirins, a glass of water, and a pot to piss in, please.* I pass another door, it's blocked off with yellow caution tape. Then another. All the room doors between the maid and the elevator are blocked off with caution tape. Whatever nonsense is in those rooms, there are probably also beds and working bathrooms.

The Device

He has swum, Eduardo Ruiz, towards the bread island in nothing but a simple pair of light-blue bathing trunks that he had preferred over trunks of the same cut in seafoam green.

He's not far from the Smoker's Garden, but towards the gulls nonetheless. The muscles in his stomach tense, cramp, spasm from the cold. The veins in his arms pulse, a visible blue. Water drips down his forehead from short black curls. Except for the chill in his eyes, the rattling in his hands and jaw, you'd think you were looking at a photograph of a summer night. He pulls at a double-braid nautical rope, hand over hand, in front of his waist.

He's standing now in water thigh deep. In the night, his eyes are blue and transparent. They look like fish bowls with a tiny black fish floating around in dye-blue water.

The rope swooshes, burns his hands in the cold water, but he keeps pulling. At the end of it is a steel cage on orange floats, shadows indicating trapped beings. It gets closer as he huffs, pauses to wipe sea and sweat from his forehead, to warm a hand in the pit of his arm, to change grips, and to do the same with the other. He stops to look at his hands, the pruned fingers, the red palms, the beginning of blistering.

"None of this is authorized," a naked gull shouts from inside the cage. "I'm not okay with this. I do not consent." Eduardo Ruiz pulls at the same pace, sees that there are three naked gulls in the cage. He's pleased. You can see him smiling through his shivers.

The cage hits mud. He has to wade further out, but the water does not get deeper. The gulls are silent, maybe praying, maybe meditating, maybe attempting soulular translocation. He takes them, binds their beaks with lobster bands, and shoves them into a satchel. Muffled voices mutter incoherent words too quiet to be heard over the wind.

With the birds in his bag, he re-baits the cage with rye bread and flings it out as far as he can.

9.

Eduardo Ruiz's congee is a hard disk. Seagulls have picked out the dried shrimp. The scallions have wilted. The soy sauce has crystallized. The ice in his glass has melted, then evaporated. He's still sitting at the head of the table with his case between his ankles. More naked gulls have gathered on and around the stone wall. There are maybe sixty now, and it stinks.

"Mr. Ruiz?"

"Yes."

"How about some water?"

"There's no water. I've been ordering some. I've drunk all they could find." He smells worse than the birds. Gray stubble is becoming a light beard. It's starting to hide the dandruff flaking from under his chin. His eyes are wet and yellow, rivered with bright red stripes. His face is cold, almost relaxed. He's as far away as Sonia was on the long-boat.

"Have you been up to your room?"

"Oh no. No. I don't have a room. It's just a day trip for the presentation to Mr. Delivan and Mr. White."

"Where did you... did you sleep here? In the garden?"

"No... no. I haven't slept. I'm just, I'm still waiting. He'll be down any minute. So they say. They keep saying."

"Do you mind if I join you?"

"Not at all. Please do." He shows an open palm. I pull out a chair. "Oh no. Not there. I'm certain they'll ask you to move. You should sit in your assigned seat. Over there, where you sat for breakfast."

"Sure. I'll sit there. No problem." I move around, passing under the green leaves that hang over Sonia's chair, tasting her perfume coming off the plant. "Has Ms. Salazar been down?"

"Oh, goddammit," I hear from near the double doors. "I'm not supposed to be on for another fifteen minutes." The peacock spits out a lit cigarette. He hops up on the table, bows, and freezes into his statue pose.

"I, we're fine, thank you. We're just chatting." He doesn't break his posture. Four doormen march out. They take their positions behind each chair. "We're fine, thank you."

"It's policy, sir. We insist," the tall one, who plays the accordion, says.

"Just ignore them, it's no use." Eduardo Ruiz taps a

spoon at the hardened congee.

"May I have a latte please, and a cigar?" I ask over my shoulder.

"I will relay your request to the desk, sir."

"They won't tell anyone about it," Eduardo says. "In a minute, they're going to bring more of that cinnamon stick coffee. Only now it's cold. I think it's all from the same batch."

"I won't drink it," I say.

"You will. We all do. It's still coffee."

"I guess it is."

"The only thing worse is no coffee at all." He thunks at his congee. "Between the two of us, I'm starting to suspect that maybe Mr. Delivan's not coming. If you don't mind my asking, is it… usual… for him to be… so late… to insist on such waiting?"

"I wish I could answer that for you. My business dealings with him are limited. I will say our transactions have always been straightforward. Did you say if Ms. Salazar had been down yet?"

"She has not, not since yesterday."

"Good morning, sir." A waiter serves a mug of coffee with a cinnamon stick. "Will the others be joining?"

"I'm not sure," I say.

"Very good, sir."

"A gull crashed into my window this morning." I turn back to Eduardo Ruiz.

"Hm."

93

"Broke the glass."

"Did he leave a note?"

"He did."

"Do you have it?"

"No, I assumed that would be an issue for the authorities."

"Hm." He slouches down, sighs, and drops the spoon to the ground. "Waiter."

"Yes, sir?"

"Bring a bottle of rum."

"As you wish."

"Why does the rum come so quick?"

"They bill for it. The water is complimentary."

"I'll pay for water. I feel like I haven't had a drop since I checked in."

"Maybe so. I wonder, would you like to see my invention?"

"He's a monster. That man is a monster," a naked gull says, and scurries, feet pitter-pattering, towards the ocean.

The others part, let him pass, then mumble amongst themselves.

"Oh, fuck off, will you, please. Jesus, these birds."

"If you'd like to show me, sure," I say. "What's your invention?" I gulp the cold coffee. The case is on the table now. Out from under his feet, the box looks like it holds some sort of horn instrument. He taps the case, searches my face. "It's not a problem. I don't need to see it. If you're worried."

94

"Maybe you can relay your thoughts to Mr. Delivan, if you see him." He opens the case. Laid inside molded foam is a metal tube. It's black, looks like a mini version of a World War mortar, complete with the tripod, the base, and something that looks like a firing mechanism.

The naked gulls squawk in a chaotic symphony. Some waddle into the mud, others jump right into the water. "You son of a bitch," one shouts.

"Animal," another. Two or three stand frozen at the stone wall. The feathered gulls, without squawking, glide off to sea, as if never having lingered above us, as if simply passing in migration to warmer climates.

"Is this a weapon?"

"No." He stands it up on the table, pointing it out to the ocean. If it were a mortar it would fire right over his shoulder. The peacock turns his eyes towards me, checking me for concern.

"It really looks like a mortar."

"It's not a weapon, but there are moral implications."

"What does it do?"

"Well, that's the thing. That's the special part." He stands up, smiles. "Look," he says, and he turns his back to me. "The naked gulls. Don't they look lost to you? Sunburned, miserable."

"I can't," the peacock says. "I'm sorry. I'm uncomfortable. Excuse me." He knocks over a coffee getting off the table.

"They're burned all up, tired. Look, they're miserable,"

95

Eduardo starts again. "They're stuck here. They don't belong here. They—I don't know where they belong, sure. I'll
admit that. But, science aside, basic observation tells you,
look at them, they're not from here, they don't belong here.
They can't even survive or thrive here. They subsist on that
disgusting bread. Have you tasted it? It's—something has to
be done. That's what I'm saying."

"I don't—"

"This device," he interrupts. "It feathers them."

"Feathers them?"

"Yes. And this isn't some glue-and-feathers variety. It
naturally feathers them. They can fly away. Eventually, I'll
do the research and figure out where it is they go. They
don't stay. There's an instinct. Something. They know
where to go. And that's the proof they don't belong here. If
they did, well, feathered or not, they'd stay right here."

"I see."

"You load a gull in here, it pops… like a mortar, as you
described, and the gull comes out feathered. With real
feathers, its own, natural feathers. Just like the gulls flying
off at sea. I want to stress, this isn't some glue-and-feathers
trick. They are real, natural feathers, and the naked gulls,
once feathered, they fly away. "

"I don't know what to make—"

"Know? No. There's nothing to know. I'm solving a
problem. That's all there is to it."

"And Mr. Delivan?"

"The issue with people like Mr. Delivan, and, I'm honestly surprised by his interest in the project, is that… well, there's no money to be made. It's more of a conservation project. My fear is… you see, the thing is, there's no money to be made as is, but the technology, that's the magic. That's what the government wants, that's what everyone wants. That's why I insisted on Ms. Salazar being here, to document, as a matter of personal safety, all of this. The technology alone is dangerous, but the conservation value is immeasurable, well, depending on your beliefs.

"Some say, and I get it quite often, that it's not our place to interfere with nature, that if the gulls want it, why do they run away, that there's nothing wrong with the gulls as is, but, I don't know about you, I remember a day when there were no naked gulls, and I can't help but feel that their condition is man-made. It's not some evolutionary thing. It's the result of man and therefore the responsibility of man to fix it."

"But they do run away, I just saw it."

"That's the other dilemma, and the one that I struggle with, personally. Once a gull is loaded, it's not a guarantee that it'll come out feathered. A good number of them, sometimes as many as seventy percent, just disappear. They climb in, the device pops, and they're gone. It's an element of the technology that neither I nor my team quite understand. But the gulls that climb in, they know the risk. They were all volunteers in the studies. Family members, flocks, were compensated generously."

"Compensated?"

"Bread, water, shelter. Yes. As you can imagine, money

is no use to a gull."

"I don't see, from my dealings with Mr. Delivan and Mr. White, why they would have any interest in this."

"That's my worry. That's why I almost left yesterday. But, the desk continues to assure me of Mr. Delivan's personal interest in further conversation, insisting on his passion for conservation."

"Pardon the interruption, gentleman." The double doors pop open. A waiter marches in rolling a snare drum. "Ms. Salazar and Mr. White."

"My lord," Sonia says. "I should hope we're not to be beheaded." The two are dressed in formal evening wear. Sonia in a red gown, Ed White in white tie.

"What's all this?" Eduardo starts packing up his device. "Is this a formal event?"

"No, darling, we've just come from a cocktail meet and greet upstairs." She looks at me. "Still in the spa get-up?"

"I guess so." I still haven't found an aspirin. *Christ, when did she get all dressed up?*

"What meet and greet? I wasn't told," Eduardo says.

"Me neither," I say.

"A media thing. Don't worry yourself."

"Ladies and gentlemen, breakfast is served." It's congee again.

The Woman

She scribbles with her pen broad unending circles until the paper gives up, allowing its surface to be tilled to lesser layers, layer by layer, turning black with each pass, holding the pen like a child might grasp a pencil, or she stabs the pen directly, forcing the damage, hastening it, hoping for the ballpoint tip to compress into the ink chamber to burst the ink chamber and splash gunshot-splatter ink over the desk or wall, or for the spring to pop and render the pen useless, or the tip to rip/divide into sharp metal pieces that cut her fingers and pattern actual blood onto the same space, but the words won't come. There are no poems on the paper, no article or journal entry, no letter home. It's empty.

And the pen will be empty too, or the paper, or everything. The only danger is nothing when she feels everything and living is in fact only the infatuation with being alive.

She's opened her door, well, unlocked it rather. She's propped it slightly by opening the door, closing the swing bar door guard (satin chrome), then allowing the door itself to rest against the door guard, opposite its purpose. Anyone could push the door, shove it or slam it or walk right in or knock in that light, friendly way you knock on a door that's already open.

The pen bursts, something has finally given out. It collapses inward, unseen, but the syrupy ink oozes over the paper, envelopes the page, touches the desk's wax-polished wood. She exhales her anxiety, and for a moment, a small moment, she is relieved and overcome with the simple desire to sleep. She thinks: *Tomorrow. Tomorrow.*

She's lying in bed now, lighting a cigarette again, and the lines race through her head, words scrambled up to mean nothing even though each one means something and all together mean something else that she doesn't understand but feels. Her hair runs over her shoulders like water under moonlight, like the trickling of a stream's casual path, splitting at her shoulder, winding into eddy currents at her collar bone, filling the ravines formed by her shoulder blades. Not knowing where it's going, not caring. *Whatever it touches will grow green, or tall, or fat, or (simply) live another day.*

She crosses her legs and glances to the door, drawn by the sliver of vertical light, or rather the quick shadow of the line itself cut off by the passing of *a figure another guest a person an animal (no, too tall)* but the shadow is gone, blinked away.

She thinks *maybe I blinked, maybe it was a blink*, and she laughs to herself thinking *I should close the door, go to sleep*. She flirts with the idea of posing, imagines herself *shredded of clothes laying flat legs crossed at the ankles or legs open cigarette at the corner of a dangerous smile or maybe she'll be at the edge of the bed back arched at the waist eyes straight at the headboard*.

She doesn't want the formalities or informalities, no chit chat or catching up or getting to know each other. She wants what she wants and then she wants him gone (*damn social norms*), left to remain in the imagination of her desire so that fantasy can stay fantasy and life can stay life and she'll never know what the bathroom smells like after he's taken a shit nor how loud he snores after drinking all night, and he'll never find the patch of rough skin behind her knee, the tiny blue veins starting at the insides of her ankles.

Or she'll wear the evening dress, black. She'll sit at the desk, papers intentionally arranged, hands washed of ink, cigarette installed in the cigarette holder, and she'll say *Hello darling, good evening, a cocktail? How about gin? Lovely, you've brought flowers. There's a vazzz there.*

She throws the cigarette at the ashtray on the desk. A miss. But there's no danger of fire, it's far from the papers. It will only melt a little polish.

She jumps off the bed, closes the door trying not to make a sound (she's thinking of the neighboring rooms and feeling embarrassed), locks it. The fantasy went away, mixing with real life when the shadow passed. So she's shut her-

101

self in to find it again.

She does find it. By practicing the poses, trying others. By smoking more cigarettes, by masturbating, playing different scenes out from far beyond her imagination from somewhere in the pit of her stomach, reaching for a version of herself that doesn't exist in this reality, but she is there somewhere, she feels that other life there's something perfect in it *who is that woman who am I I can feel her where are you and who is it that gives us this*. She orgasms, breathes, and it's all gone again.

The air conditioner is rattling.

10.

Pudge uses the edge of a new bowl to discreetly scoot away Eduardo Ruiz's dried-up dish. He checks my eyes for a reaction, and I cringe. Then he shrugs and edges the bowl off the end of the table like a cat might do. The old congee holds everything together, and the unbroken ceramic bounces with a low hum.

"Just take it away, man," I say. "Not everything has to be weird." Pudge says nothing. One of the doormen is already sweeping up the bowl while the others settle into their places behind our chairs. The sweeper is having a hard time with the bowl, as it didn't break, so the broom's straws sort of, like, brush at it.

I'm surprised to see my guy stumbling through the double doors in a Mr. Bean sort of way, making Mr. Bean sort of eyes. He takes his place behind my chair and is completely impressed with himself. This may be the first time he's made it to a meal service. Pudge steps backward three large steps and takes his own place as the supervisor/conductor of this breakfast.

Eduardo, looking into his fresh bowl, reaches for the condiments and starts loading it up with dried shrimp. "Oh come on. Please, not this again," I say. Eduardo says nothing. He's back in that lost trance. "Look at the other one. He can't even sweep it up."

"Let the man eat, darling."

"He's ruining this one too," I say, putting a prawn to my mouth. "He didn't touch the last one. It's a brick. Look at it."

"Please, not this again, darling."

"Are we getting the bottle of rum?" Ed White searches the table. I can't help but think he's looking for a plate of cold cuts. "Hey, where's the rooster thing?"

"Peacock, darling."

"Oh right. My father used to raise them."

"You told us."

"There's rum on the table."

"Eduardo, you alright there, buddy? You look about hypnotized by that porridge." Ed White grins. He's staring at Sonia while he speaks. "You ain't still worried about Mr. Delivan. He'll be down. Don't worry a bit."

"You know darling, maybe we *should* consider mojitos again."

There's the wooden creak of the double doors being

cracked open, revealing an eye, half of a face. The doormen look at Pudge who bows to us and marches to the cracked door. No one takes any interest except for me and Eduardo, who has stood up. Pudge is whispering through the door, "Well yes…. understand… can wait until…. there is an itinerary… yes I…"

"Well, you've done it now," Pudge says. Eduardo grabs his case, high steps towards the ocean. The few gulls still hanging around waddle or fly off (based on their feather status). "You've totally ruined the breakfast program." Pudge pulls the double doors open.

Two men in olive military drab peddle in on a tandem bicycle. They're wearing tall, neatly polished cognac boots, and what I can only describe as red-dyed Red-Army-style military fur cossacks emblazoned with what I think is a palm tree emblem. The bicycle itself is a freshly polished fire engine red.

Eduardo Ruiz steps over the stone wall and wades out into the water, holding the case over his head, glancing forward, backward, forward again, whimpering. "The sun must be getting to him," Ed White says. "Should we save his plate?"

"No, darling. He's fine, I'm sure."

The tandem cyclists ring the bell. It's one of those kids' rotating bicycle bells. They come down the steps much more gracefully than I ever could have imagined. Then they circle the table twice, ringing the bell periodically, and come to a stop at the head seat. Without dismounting the bicycle, they, in unison, plant their left feet on the ground and point their left arms straight forward to balance so that they're leaning towards the table, almost in an uprock breakdancing pose.

"Sir, you," the pedal guard at the back of the bicycle says.

"Yes?" Ed white responds, starts to stand.

"No," the handlebar guard says, involuntarily wiggling the bars and destabilizing the tandem.

"Sir, you," Pedal says again.

"Yes?" I say.

"You, yes. We've…. Are you Eduardo Ruiz?"

"No."

"Which one are you?"

"That's our itinerary change," Pedal says.

"Oh, I see. Yes. We've been advised of your intent to alter your official itinerary," Handlebars says. Pedal squints out towards Eduardo while trying to look like he's not trying to look for Eduardo. I suspect Pedal doesn't want to be the only person of official capacity, nor the first one, to notice that a man has fled the scene.

"My goodness, how official, darlings."

"Do not interrupt the King's Guard."

Sonia wobbles her head, salutes. There's a smirk at the corner of Pudge's mouth. He's standing there behind this whole situation, half annoyed, half amused. I suspect he's hoping for my arrest if that's within the scope of the law for this interaction.

"That's corr—" I start.

"DO NOT INTERRUPT THE KING'S GUARD!" They stomp their feet in unison.

Man, they take themselves seriously. I've lost interest. It's going to be hard to listen to these guys.

"The authorities have been advised of your intent to alter your official itinerary."

Shit, I missed that. They used the word "official," and that's not a good sign. I look over at Pudge. If these guys don't arrest me, that fat son of a bitch will fill me in. He has to. Surely, it's part of his job. I could leave a bad review. No hotel wants that. Not even a secret one.

"You are required to submit to a formal exit interview."

"It's pretty informal, actually," Pedal says, still watching Eduardo. Handlebars winces.

"You are required to submit to a FORMAL exit interview. Your interview time is scheduled for one hour and forty-five minutes after the approval of your exit application."

Oh, I forgot about the ice apprentice. Man, that was a show. I saw him working last night when I went to pee off the roof. Remind me to tell you about that.

Actually, I'll tell you now, I don't want to oversell it. So, he is in fact an apprentice to a Master Ice whatever from wherever, Japan. He is working here illegally. There is something about an illegitimate child or a gambling debt or an addiction to something. I didn't quite understand. But, here is the interesting part, he uses moon water to make his ice.

107

He takes regular water, and (as I understand it) ages it under moonlight to absorb the magical moon powers from the gods of whatever. I didn't taste anything special in the ice, but that's it. That's the part about the ice.

"In the event that your application is not approved, your exit interview will be canceled and you will be subjected to a twenty dollar fee. The location of your interview will be provided upon approval of your application. You may *now* comment or question the King's Guard."

Did he say 'twenty dollars'? "Is that twenty U.S. dollars? I haven't submitted my application yet."

Pedal and Handlebars exchange glances. Pudge marches over, and the three start whispering amongst themselves. Then without another word, they peddle off, first ringing their bell, then making three ceremonial circles around the table (nearly falling over when the front wheel touches a decorative rock), then up the stairs, back through the double doors, presumably through the hotel lobby, and to who knows where.

"Well, that was weird," Ed White says, breaking the moment of frozen silence.

"He didn't answer my question."

"Strange indeed, darling. The talk of the king, is there a king here? I missed that."

"Mm," Ed says. "The porridge is amazing today. Taste that butter. My Goodness."

"I didn't know they have a king. You think that fine is in U.S. dollars? I didn't bring any cash."

"To be quite honest, darling, there are days I have no idea where I am at all."

"I'll spot you the twenty if you end up needing it," Ed says.

"Thanks Ed," I say. He nods. "Imagine taking a government so seriously that you dress up like that and ride that stupid bicycle. All that and the whole world has no idea any of you exist."

"I thought it was charming, darling."

"Oh, Eduardo is still out there," Ed says. Eduardo's head is popping up between waves. Even though he's far out now, you can feel his eyes examining the Smoker's Garden, our expressions, counting bodies, trying to calculate what all is going on over here, why the King's men are sniffing around.

"I think he's waving, darling." Sonia stands up and squints her eyes, shielding them with a saluted hand. "Yes, he's waving."

"Does he need help?"

"Waiter." She squints harder. "Some binoculars, please."

"Right away, madam."

"No, no. He's fine. I think he's smiling. He's just waving. Yoohoo," she says. "Yoohoo!" She waves.

The sea wants to swell. I can see her rising, her glow becoming green. Eduardo Ruiz floats, or bobs rather, like a shipwrecked sailor making his way to a raft. He's holding the case in one hand now, pointing that arm straight above

109

his head. She's right, he does seem to be waving.

It's here that Pudge notices a discrepancy in the head count. He's the second person of official capacity to realize a man has fled the scene. The doormen sense his vibe and look nervous, twitching their fingers, side glancing at each other.

"Oh, oh I see," Eduardo's doorman says. "It's my dude. He's, uhm… made a run for it?"

Pudge whispers into the doorman's ear. He leans over and whispers to the next guy, etc, etc. They stomp once, step back twice, and march away towards the water.

A few minutes pass, and the men reappear in the longboat, starting the chug towards the banana bread. Eduardo starts swimming, now with a purpose.

"Maybe he is in trouble," Ed White says.

"They'll fish him out of there, darling, don't worry."

Orgy Floor

They can't touch anything but they can feel everything and the hormones hit the receptors, and the vision is so real they don't need to really feel because the mind fills in the physical touches to avoid the self-destruction that would follow the realization that none of this is actually real, just technology, chemistry, the perfect maximum doses of all the right hormones to hit the exact receptors to take the subject to the verge of collapse.

It is Doritos® for the senses designed by experts. Maximum doses of fat, sugar, salt to trigger every response to make you buy the fucking chips until your heart explodes.

We used to be iPhone zombies, now we're just zombies chasing dings, likes, clicks, buzzes, alerts, 3-second videos, reading poems ten words long, scrolling for hours, pinging the brain, and we all want to be influencers, and it was the

Devil who invented the front-facing camera if the Devil were real.

The room is black. It's quiet except for his deep breaths. He's almost flat in the recliner, and his position indicates that it feels like something between the stiffness of a dentist chair before a drilling and the inviting comfort of a sofa bed. The headset is large. It's almost like a motorcycle helmet. It's connected to a thick cable that connects to the ceiling and runs to a central processor. Data collected and sold to help sellers later sell more shit to you to keep you distracted from noticing you're not a human being anymore, and nature is long gone, and so is basic living, and your fresh air is a TikTok of a hiker, and the sun shines through IG reels, and the sex is digital even at a clandestine orgy.

11.

"He's almost to the island. Look how hard he's swimming." Ed White drops his head, adjusts it side to side, trying for a better view. There's a strange air over the garden, something almost too calm, punctuated by the hollow pulsing, puttering depression of empty keys as the accordionist fiddles with his instrument in a pattern meant to kill time. He's leaning against a wall, inconspicuously chatting with the peacock. Their voices sound like whomping.

Sonia, having mostly lost interest, is poking small holes in her food with her fork then smoothing them out with the back of her spoon. Her eyes trace words in the horizon.

"I'm going to find Mr. Delivan. He should be updated." Ed White straightens his shirt out as he stands, pauses/ducks at the swoop of a gull the way one might avoid a wasp, then straightens his shirt some more, and leaves.

The gull stays, hovers, dives, hovers again. There are no fish to be caught, but he's still searching, or he's sending us some sort of message, or he's hunting us. He's abandoned the figure eight, reconvened with nature, opening his beak, closing it, snapping for tiny fish, returning to a primitive instinct that flirts with leftist rebellion in the full circle come back to center. If he could laugh he would, while the other feathered gulls watched, struggling to keep their figure eight (which would have gone off center from their heads turning).

The peacock leaves behind the accordion man and returns to his role, barely announcing his arrival by clearing his throat. I hear the splashing of distant waves where Eduardo pushes water using cupped hands that have been taking turns holding the case.

Pudge is on his knees wiping away tire tracks at the tile near the double doors. The tandem bicycle men were sloppier with their exit than I had realized. It's a snake pattern they left behind. It seems everyone is smoothing something out, a shirt, words fluttering in the mind, the ocean herself.

"Well, darling, maybe they *are* after him for that thing. I guess I'll be leaving too. Everyone is preoccupied."

Stay for a drink, let's talk about something. Tell me why you've been coming to my room at night when I'm asleep. Are we in love? She's standing up, arranging the cigarette holder at the corner of her smile. Her eyes are on me, and I want to say something. I want to say everything, but there's nothing to say in real life where words and actions are ruled by etiquette and norms. "Okay," I say.

"I'll see you at dinner, I'm sure of it. Please let me know what becomes of Mr. Ruiz."

"I will."

"Something about us damned souls," she says. "There's an understanding."

"It's the gossip. Our demons drink at the same bars."

"Yes, exactly. Ciao, darling."

"Bye," I'm able to get out in a whisper. I should have said "ciao" too. I should have said anything. She's gone.

"Pudge, is the mimosa station open?"

"Have at it," he says, scrubbing the floor, now wearing a yellow hazmat suit with green rubber boots. I mix up a mimosa with the blood orange. Fuck it, I think. I'm thirsty. I down one, mix up a refill. I down another. The sugar sticks to my teeth.

"Just take your seat, man." Pudge shakes himself to standing, pulls off the hazmat hood. He carries the juice fountain to the table with a grunt, thump, and the rolling splash of a juice wave that won't be cleaned up. Then he brings two bottles of champagne with their labels scraped off to white sticker lines.

"I guess you might as well join me, Pudge."

"Sure, why not?" He sees me looking at the bottles. "It's a copyright thing, the labels." He snaps the rag. "We tried to get a sponsor, but no takers. And the lawyers were worried about associating with alcohol branding."

"But a Smoker's Garden is okay?"

115

"Why not? It's generic. It used to be the Virginia Slims Menthol Garden, but we lost the licensing." He squeezes the rag, stares over at the tire tracks.

"Don't you have people for that? The cleaning?" I slouch into my chair, feeling heavy. Regretting inviting this asshole to converse. But what else am I going to do? Go to my room and sit alone rolling over all the things I could have said or will say later to Sonia Salazar who maybe doesn't know I exist in a life outside of being a warm body? Call down the desk for a red glow-parrot and fill pages to toss in the bin?

"We're all volunteers here." He finally sits. He's more smug than he was when he was lounging in the elephant chair. Now that I think about the lobby, I should try to go again. Even with all those mimosas, I'm still dead thirsty. It must be the air here, something like that, that sucks away your moisture. If I leave Pudge sitting, I could try for the lobby, or I can wait for the next distraction. I've never gone this long being clogged up. I guess I should be considering medical care, antibiotics. But that doesn't feel like the right option here.

"Those men, they weren't here about your packet." Pudge's eyes light up. He also droops down in his chair, matching my own body language. "They're after your other friend. The one that made a run for it."

"Jesus, you think? I hadn't figured that out."

"He's overstayed his visa."

"This is all really interesting. Pudge, tell me. Where is

116

Mr. Delivan?"

"How should I know?"

"Pudge."

"In his suite, where he's been the whole time."

"What's the deal here?"

"What deal? Everything is compliments of Mr. Delivan. That congee is flown in from China. Kaito went to great lengths to get it here. He's not even Chinese, you know."

"The ice man?"

"He does a lot more than ice."

"Like what?"

"He brought all the congee. Do you have any idea what it's like getting something like that, and in that quantity mind you, not only out of China, but through all the borders, Customs, inspections, the King's Guard, everything it takes to get here? It's no joke."

"I see."

Past the double doors, a red carpet (the kind celebrities use to celebrate themselves) runs the length of the hallway that leads to the elevator, but it celebrates nothing. It's dull like old blood, and it ends suddenly with gold flag tassels over a white marble tile floor. Continue straight towards the lobby desk, then pass the desk to four vintage orange floral armchairs, a coffee table, and yesterday's newspaper. Pass the brass bellhop luggage cart, and through the next double doors there's the main hotel doors. They're hand carved by an artisan from a different age. Out on the patio it's orange tile in a geometric Moroccan style. Pass the black wrought iron bench where Warhol used to smoke (so they say), to the blacktop street, down the hill to another hill that raises to a seaview to the road, an actual concrete road where taxis never pass, or take a sharp left to elevators with brass doors, press the soup for the floor you want, and stay.

Pudge drones on, and I follow the path with Sonia as if we're walking arm in arm, but she's alone standing at the gold tassels, looking in front of her and playing out the same route in her mind, flagging a taxi, finding a ferry, going. Or she turns left, presses the button, finds her room. And life continues.

The Woman

It's morning. The room is empty, but it's not quiet. It's loud, too loud even, and her head is pounding from not sleeping. She needs water, wants water, but she's drinking coffee she made from vacuum sealed grounds with bathroom tap water in the four-cup drip machine next to the plastic cups wrapped in plastic film for cleanliness. *It's the perfect breakfast*, she thinks, despite the cliché. She dips the filtered end into her coffee. *Why not?* She thinks. *No one is watching. No one is here. It's just me, and it's all too quiet for so much noise.*

Slow taxis honk at slower taxis slowing for pedestrians insisting on their right to the crosswalk when the light is flashing that only seven more seconds remain. In some countries, they just swoop around, but rules are rules and the rules here are to wait.

119

The sun hurts and she considers *a migraine another hour of sleep delaying again a glass of water for the excuse I have a headache.* Delaying the whole day for tomorrow because *what does it matter anyway one day I'll forget all of this* (she thinks) *before I was born there was nothing and I knew nothing not even existence and now I exist to ends unknown but infinitely assigned tasks unimportant for the purpose of participation in this contract with whom exactly I don't need work to live. I don't need money. I need food, water, love, shelter, and all of those things are illegal in one way or the other unless you find them by the rules. Hunt without a license. Pick berries on public land. Collect rainwater, fish in the stream, sleep in the sand. No, they won't allow it. They won't allow it for more than a few days.*

Man owns the land, the labor, our bodies and the gods own the souls, but man really owns the souls too because it's the fruit the promise of what the gods give later that keeps all in line now playing by man's rules in man's land from which he came but turns his back to.

The sun hits the window, touches the dust in the air, and she sips her coffee, now lukewarm, lights another cigarette looking at the red plaque with white letters that says "No Smoking," another small rebellion that no one knows about but her. And when she puts her head down, leaning slightly against the chair, the cold fabric chilled by air conditioning touches the left side of her face, eyes closed. She feels skin, it's soft, it's warm but cold too. *Soft.*

In her mind, *it's mother's breast a heart beating beneath warm skin chilled by the open air of exposed natural love instinctual love to raise a child from nothing. The sweat of her skin is her mother's on the arm of the chair.* She closes her eyes and everything can be al-

120

right, but it's not alright, and her eyes swell, redden but she won't cry. No, she won't let herself cry. *Not for a chair. Not for a memory an idea a sentiment of what should be but isn't and never can be again.*

She stands. The day is coming.

122

12.

The Norwegian woman, in a white dress with her legs crossed, waits in the elevator corridor. She taps the toe box of one beige high heel against the heel of the other to an unpatterned beat. Candles light a path in the hall towards the Smoker's Garden. A few unfamiliar voices drift our way.

In the lobby, it's dark too. Sticks is clacking away at the Remington Portable. The two tandem guards sit having coffee or beer with their bicycle propped up against the wall.

The elevator dings. I start back to my room to clear my head. I plan to lie down, turn the lights off, force some silence, force calm, to lie in bed without moving, to stop time, to reset, to try again later. The Norwegian woman gestures to indicate she won't be boarding the same elevator as me. As the floors roll by, I catch myself cursing out to nobody.

Or to everybody and everything.

The walk to my room is a blur, and at my door the candle struggles with its last light, then drowns away in the hot wax. A puff of black smoke scented by charred wick. The doorman forgets his greeting. Instead, he side glances at my hand turning the knob, and I enter into a room filled with anxiety and stale air, absent of human existence.

Then I see it. They've taken the bed. The floor is two or three shades brighter where the bed was. All of the bedding is piled (yes piled, not folded) on the seat of the armchair with the pillows resting on top like the cherry. It's an apartment before the last load to the truck on moving day. It's the old chair that's being left behind, the sheets that will be used to wrap furniture or otherwise thrown out. But they've fixed the window, installed new glass so clear it's not there. I hold my fingers to it, smear a print into its face, then another. Now it's there, overlooking the sea. Outside it's winter gray, early morning quiet. The sea sways not roars.

This is unacceptable.

I shove the door open.

"Where's the damn bed?" My shout gives my doorman a start, and I suddenly know he'd been waiting for this.

"It's being cleaned, sir," he mumbles. "A safety precaution, glass fragments." He snaps his heels.

"Where am I supposed to sleep? This is unacceptable. The most unprofessional hotel experience I can remember." I feel my feet pacing the space between my room and the hallway.

"A fresh mattress will be up for you shortly, sir." His posture drops.

"How long?"

"Perhaps a drink in the Smoker's Garden would relax you, sir?" He almost points, his arm hovering between an attention pose and offering a leading-me-by-the-hand gesture.

"How long until the bed is back?"

"Not long, sir." He's back at attention. "Maybe a cocktail in the lobby?"

"I just came from there. What about a glow-parrot? Can I get a red one?"

"Yes, sir."

"Make sure it's sent up. Please. I have so much to do."

"Yes, sir."

"Jesus." I slam the door. I move around the room, nearly stomping, searching the bright spot of floor where the bed had been for some sort of answer. There isn't one. Just old sun through a fresh window, a pile of bedding, and nowhere to sleep.

I push the bedding from the armchair, and I plop in. The scroll, the note from the gull, is there on the desk. I'm surprised the authorities didn't take it. I go back and throw the door open again, giving the doorman another start.

"They left the note, from the gull. They forgot it," I say.

"Yes sir, it's addressed to you, sir."

I don't know what to say. I slam the door again. The

scroll is light in my hand, smells like park birds. I'm more inclined to drop it in the trash, but it is addressed to me. There's even a gold wax seal, well, more yellow than gold, but still formal. I open it up.

Thin black ink: "Here I am. Here I was. There you are."

Hm, I think. *That's dumb.* There's a knock. "Come in," I say.

"Ladies and Gentlemen, Ms. Sonia Salazar," my doorman announces.

Jesus, I've got to get out of here. "Hello Sonia."

"How about a drink, darling?" She lowers a dark pair of sunglasses. "My god, what is this? I swear you had a bed here."

"They're cleaning it." A glow-parrot flies in and takes his position on the light fixture. It's a blue one.

"Oh, well, how nice. I love blue. How about a drink? Everyone's gathering downstairs for a pregame."

"We just came from there."

"That was hours ago. Tell me you're not losing it. My goodness everyone around here is totally losing it."

"I'm staying in."

"Don't be that way, darling. The night is young, as they say."

"All the same."

"If you change your mind." She almost bows, taking her exit. *What a play this has been,* I think. I lay on the bright spot of floor, close my eyes, and think about stopping time.

The glowing blue penetrates my shut eyelids.

There is the option of the lobby bathroom. Pudge did offer it as a room, but it doesn't take much imagination to see that there are more dashes in the cons column than in the pros.

I think it's probably a safe time to tell you that Tony Soprano and his Goomah from season two actually were staying on the same floor as me. Except it wasn't TS. At least, not TS as portrayed by James Gandolfini. It was a different actor. Some B-list guy. And it was all blurry. By that I mean I dreamed that TS and his Goomah from season 2 were staying on the same floor as me. We met at the elevator headed for the lobby bathroom. Pudge was there, playing night watchman. When we entered, he held out a blue, plastic beach pail. TS shrugged and dropped his penis into the bucket. I looked inside, it was full of penises.

"I'm afraid you must check your member, sir," Pudge said.

"I see," I said, and obliged. I took the urinal next to TS, we both tried to pee, but we couldn't. We shared a shrug, and a smile. *Some rules make no sense.*

Orgy Floor

He's not expected to make it out alive.

13.

I wake up in the navy dusk of indistinguishable water and sky, and there she is, cozy and innocent, the woman no one else sees, but for some reason she's showing herself to me. The sun comes in the same way as before, illuminating her exposed legs. They're flawless. I hadn't heard or felt her come in, again, and it wasn't cold last night, but I guess I don't mind. I'll take the attention during my unconscious hours, even if that means only getting to absorb it all passively. That part is over now, once our eyes open to real life. When the cracks show in the walls of consciousness.

She's stirring with apparent comfort despite having slept on the bare floor, a single pillow and a single white sheet between the two of us. My back hurts from the same. Long itching red lines run down my legs and pattern my arm too. I sneak over to the armchair, but I won't stare at her. I won't watch her. I won't be the longing man dreaming of a life that isn't his because the dream is over. The glow-parrot is gone. It's a ray of sun touching the edges of morning reality.

I'll sit in the chair, close my eyes again. I'll listen to the creaking leather or vinyl upholstery (whatever it is) that sticks to the back of my legs. I'll close my eyes and burst through the ceiling, flap my wings like the gulls, fly to wherever they fly, join the figure eight pattern, be.

She opens her eyes. I pull my robe closed.

"Good morning, darling." She stretches her arms straight in front of her, and her elbows pop. "When did you get up? I was going to be out of here before you got up. I hope I didn't disturb you."

"Not that long ago."

"I really hope I didn't disturb you, darling. It was just so cold again. This place is so cold. I can barely stand it. I absolutely cannot stand it." She flicks the sheet away, scoots herself back so that she's sitting up with the pillow between her and the wall, her legs straight out.

"I don't mind you coming."

"Of course not. Why would you mind? If I thought you'd mind, don't you think I'd know not to bother coming?"

"I mean, you can wake me up."

"Oh no. You are absolutely so much warmer when you're out."

I don't know what to say. She's right. If she'd been waking me up, I wouldn't even try to sleep. I'd watch her with the disbelief of a child sighting a wild animal.

"Come sit with me, darling. We have a few minutes before we're due anywhere."

"Are we due somewhere?" I can't sit with her, the dream is over. It never really happened.

"They say Mr. Delivan arranged lobster."

"For breakfast?"

"Why not? Tell me you've had lobster for breakfast."

"No, I don't think I've had lobster but once or twice." My voice feels scratchy and hoarse. I imagine I sound gloomy.

"What a travesty, darling," she says, sitting up, half smiling, half smirking.

"I don't think I'd like lobster for breakfast. Don't you think it's extravagant?"

"If it's extravagant, let it be extravagant. Surely, we've earned a small treat." She's rising now, collecting herself. A sudden discomfort begins to cover her smile, but her smile's trying to show through it.

"For what?"

"Don't be that way." The smile drops away now, and she crosses her arms.

"Have you ever noticed you're surrounded by people who tell you only what they think you want to hear?"

"Is that what you think?"

"What if I told you you won't be beautiful forever?"

"Then I'd think you're cruel."

133

"That you won't be smart forever, or that you're actually not a genius, but a pretty average talent in the grand scheme of things, that you won't remember any of this and most likely the world will never remember you? That there is nothing special about you or more valuable about you than any of the other billions of humans living their lives. What if I tell you all the yes men and yes women will forget you as quickly as your talents becomes irrelevant to the next best thing and that skipping the reservation line at a restaurant doesn't mean anything to anyone, and that in fact, that might be the one real perk you have: eating first."

"You need to go." She wraps herself in the sheet.

"Go where? There's nowhere to go. We're all trapped here. In this life, in this routine, in everything."

"Swim away for all I care. Just leave."

"What if I tell you that I'm saying all of this to love you?"

"How is that love?" She moves to the door, gathering a pair of black heels I hadn't noticed.

"To tell you I love you for you. Not for any of that, any of this. The pictures in the magazines. Just you, a woman, a normal woman who could have been anybody, but you're somebody and despite that somebody I still love the nobody."

"You don't even know me."

"Don't I though? Doesn't everyone?"

"I need to go," she says, letting the sheets fall. "I'll go."

The slam of the door and the doorman's formalities

echo over the silence, then the room is quiet again. I'm alone again, but was I ever… accompanied?

I'm told I was born alone. But I know my mother was there, my father too, a doctor, a nurse. We're all born alone and we all die alone, exercising these two sacraments in our consciousness or lack of consciousness, and I wonder if we're ever not alone. My head contains one voice, my heart one beat. There is no one else in there. Is there an antonym to "alone"? If there is, I don't know it.

Naked Gulls

He's praying in Latin, but they're not Christian prayers. It's an old tradition, whatever it is he's doing, and he seems so perfect at doing it in the gold-embroidered green chasuble borrowed from the Catholics, swinging his arm, bowing, chanting. You can see all of religion in his motions. All of spirituality is encapsulated in his movements; the clicks of the brass chain against the gold-plated brass thurible; the pieces of ocean touching his sea boots, slipping away, returning; the flickering sunlight; the cloud-covered visions; the blurring of water, fog, and horizon; the trickle of blood running from the crease of his index and middle fingers, dropping into the water, and disappearing into nothing. It's all there, and the naked gulls watch, captivated as if it were all a performance.

Incense plumes upwards in bite-sized puffs, and the

137

naked gulls suck it in. They're gobbling at the bread too, dipping their beaks in the water. A few have lost interest, distracted by the flopping of a skipjack that's been caught on the dune in a recession too shallow to swim out of, too deep to die in. The birds don't eat him; they don't know how, but the urge to bite grows in their bellies.

A feathered gull dives, apparently emboldened by the naked gulls' inability to act. The naked gulls scatter, taking steps backward but watching, studying the feathered gull, but he's frozen too. The fish is too big.

So he lands, watches the tuna, exchanges glances with the naked gulls, smells the incense, feels a jolt of panic at the sudden hushing of the clicking chain as the fat boy stops swinging the thurible to see what will happen between the gulls and the tuna.

He flies away. The naked gulls move in again to examine the fish. The fat boy starts again with the incense. "It's alright. There's plenty of bread. Leave the thing alone. I'll drag it back when the ceremony is over. Eat the bread. Everything is fine."

14.

Another day is gone, and I don't remember it. I wake up alone on the floor to a muffled conversation outside my door, not knowing if it's a new day or later in the same or a repeat. It's Eduardo. "No, listen," he's saying. "I don't want to be announced. I don't want—look, take the money, and let me knock on the door. It can't be a whole— that's U.S. dollars. That's a lot of money for you people."

"Eduardo," I say. "Hold on, I'm coming." I open the door. The doorman snaps his heels.

"Ladies and gentlemen, Mr. Eduardo Ruiz."

"Christ, I just—what is wrong with—"

"Come in, Eduardo. Don't bother with him."

"I gave him twenty bucks, man." He turns back, insulted or humiliated. I don't know which. "U.S. bucks."

"Come in," I say again.

He pauses a step past the threshold. "Is this all?" It's finally occurred to him. "Where's your…. this is a closet with a window. You've been sleeping here?"

"I have a desk. I'm working on my checkout packet." I point to the stack of papers. I'm on page twenty-seven.

"I'm still waiting for mine. Maybe I gummed that up in the garden."

"It's a joke. It's got to be a joke," I say.

"Look," he hands me the device in its case. "You're gonna have to hold on to this for me."

"Why's that?" I take the chair. *Man, why didn't I sleep in the chair?* It would have made so much more sense to have slept in the chair. But I slept on the floor like a fucking idiot. It's the routine. I'm so embedded in the routine that I drop down on a bare floor because that is where the bed is supposed to be, that is where the nightstand is, that is where I'm supposed to sleep. It's been arranged. It's all been arranged.

"I need to get outta here. The lady's gone. Mr. Delivan's a no-show. It's getting dangerous. Those bicycle guys are after me."

"Sonia's gone?"

"I haven't seen Ed White either. It's all too fishy. I can't take it. They're gonna kill me. I can feel it."

"When did Sonia leave? Who told you that?"

"Who?"

"Sonia. Ms. Salazar? The journalist." I stand up, tie my spa robe.

140

"Oh, yes. The lady. She split. I thought you split too. I knocked yesterday, three times at your door. I thought you split too."

"'The Lady'? Eduardo, you're losing it, man. I think you need to calm down. What day is it? You came yesterday?"

"It's not right. It's all messed up."

"Sit down in the chair. Catch your breath." I move out of the way, point to the chair. "Sit. Just for a minute. You'll feel better. What day is it?"

"No, I need to go. Take the device. Just hold on to it for a few days, please. Until I know it's safe."

"I think you should reconsider."

"Reconsider what?"

"At least sit down a minute. Think. How are you 'getting out of here'? Did you consider that? I'm twenty-seven pages into a hundred-some page packet. You don't even have yours. This place is no joke. They'll stop you at the airport, Customs, Immigration, whatever. We're trapped here. Maybe forever. Those bicycle guys will hunt you down. You said it yourself, they're looking for you."

"That's why I'm paddlin' out, man."

"Paddling out?"

"I'm going to steal a boat and get gone."

"Jesus."

"You've seen them, the fishing boats that drop off the prawns every morning. Not the longboat, the fishing boats with the motors. I'm going to steal one. What are they going to do? Chase me in the longboat again? I'll paddle until I'm out of hearing, crank up the engine, and I'm gone."

"To where, Eduardo?"

"I'll figure it out." He leaves, turning to slam the door, but his hand catches air since the doorman is already closing it. "Jesus, man."

I drop back into the chair, my eyes on the black box, then I notice a feathered gull is hovering by the window, nodding his head as if to say *open the window*. He's got a scroll. *I'm glad he didn't smash the window*, I think. The main window doesn't open, but there's a small one to the side of the desk. I pull it open, and the gull comes in. He drops the scroll on the desk, bows, and then flies off again.

The scroll reads: "They've all gone. Myself included. -Del."

Orgy Floor

The recliner is completely flat, and his breathing is shallow. An amount of drool, nickel-sized, sticks to his mouth's corner. His fingers, with his arms straight against his sides, twitch. He knows this isn't real, and a voice further down asks: *is any of this real?* But the sensations overwhelm. He knows that voice is there, he can feel it in the milliseconds of quiet between frames, but he can't hear it. He'll be lost. Forever doped under a motorcycle headset and seven-second stimuli. If he can reach the cable, he can escape. If he can know he needs escape, he can escape. But the trap is keeping the captive perpetually in bliss, scrolling.

In this game, you earn coins. You use those coins to buy upgrades to then get more coins which you spend on variations in the seven-second stimuli. He reaches towards the cord (so he thinks) but his hand, his arm don't move. His fingers twitch, then relax, then twitch again, and he exhales a sort of grunt like he's lost his breath.

The colors in the headset are intense. You can see light refracting at the edges of the helmet. A photo right now would make a cool album cover. Light shooting off the eyes, a motorcycle helmet, a black room with blurry, fading edges. You'd want to take the picture from above looking down.

White text: "This is How it Ends" arching over the top. Bottom right: "The End" (that's the name of the band).

He's reaching, and his hand is locking up like a claw. It's the left one that's moving, and when it starts to actually lift, an outside force pushes it back down like weight in a dream. The outside force pulls him further out, and he raises his forearm at the elbow. The outside force is a human hand pushing at his forearm. He strains against the weight, a vein pops out, perspiration runs down his arm. The headset comes up.

"A break, sir?"

"No. Thank you. I'm done."

"There's so much more to see, sir."

"I'm sure."

"A small break, and we'll try again."

"No, thank you. I'm—I'll have a drink. Point me to the bar. I'm disoriented."

"Allow me." He offers an arm.

He's shaking coming out of the chair, sweating. His vision is blurry in that transition from bright to dark. As he is

144

led from the private room, he sees another private room, the light refracting from the edges of a helmet, a hand clenching at a person's side, and he laughs.

He takes a seat at the bar, taps two fingers on the bar top. The bartender glances over at him, nods. He's holding a bottle of mezcal. The two exchange more nods, and the bartender pours the shot. His hand closes around the shot glass, but he can't grasp it, and he thinks *how easy it would be to put the headset back on*.

146

15.

Pudge looks like shit. Bags under his eyes, he's two days unshaven, his uniform is disheveled and dirty like he's slept in it. He's behind the desk, slumped down so that only his head is showing, and his expression is that of a green-hued decapitated head with its tongue hanging out. *It might actually just be his head on the desk*, I think, and I stick out a finger to poke it. He doesn't respond. I poke again, dragging my finger over his lips like I'm doing the TikTok barber prank. He jumps.

"Oh no. Not you," he says. "Not right now. Not you."

"What's wrong with you? Man, where'd you find that chair?" It's a too short, duct-tape-patched, black vinyl desk chair on plastic rollers.

"I didn't sleep. Problems with—"

"That chair is wild, Pudge."

147

"It's vintage, from the 90s. Do you know what sort of problems we're dealing with?"

"Where did everyone go?" I don't care about his problems. "It's not vintage. It's trash. The guts are coming out. That foam probably causes cancer."

"It's a thing with the gulls. Everything is changing. They're all riled up about something. No one can reach Mr. Delivan. It's a mess."

"Did Ms. Salazar check out?"

"It's perfectly safe, certified by the government." His eyes are watery, red.

"Did she leave or not? Come on, Pudge." I put my weight on the counter, planting my palms flat.

"Everyone's gone. You're the only one here." He slumps further down in his chair, his voice falters, and he brushes at the exposed sections of foam. "It's just you and that lady from the non-smoker's group."

I'm disoriented. The lobby feels like it's both shrinking and disappearing, and I'm going with it one way or the other. Maybe that's life altogether, the sensation of disappearing little by little into absolutely nothing like a speck of dust passing in a blip of light. There's a whomping in my ears like you get from a hangover, but I'm not hungover. I'm still plain old thirsty.

"Pudge, call me a car, man." A panic builds in my chest. I look towards the lobby door. The fire engine red tandem is resting on its kickstand, unoccupied.

"I need your packet."

148

"Call me a car. Everyone is gone." I want to run. The front doors catch my eyes again, and I can picture myself smashing through them, leaving crumbs and splinters in my path and a perfect cartoon silhouette of myself, arms and legs extended, the glass hovering in mid-air, suspended for only a second, just a second, just long enough for you to register the speed, then it falls and shatters with cymbals crashing somewhere offstage, my hand then reaches back inside, pulls the bicycle away (with my body out of view), then you hear the sound of squeaky gears. A flashing red light alerts the live studio audience to "LAUGH."

"I can't. I can't call you a car. I can't call anyone a car. I need a code from your packet which has to be issued from above so that you can then have an exit interview." He points to the abandoned tandem. "Without a code there's no interview. Without the interview there's no car. There's no outside line to even try calling one. Please, go work on your packet. I don't know what else to do. Please, work on your packet."

"Pudge, this isn't right." I lift and slam my palms against the desk.

"No, nothing is right." He spins the chair around and starts scooting himself, his toes moving like inchworms, towards the private office.

"Are you serious?" He doesn't respond. He just scoots. Once he's in, he turns back around. He sits in the doorway looking at me, blank faced, eyes redder and redder. "What's wrong with you?"

"Time for my break," he says and closes the door. He's left a pack of cigarettes on the desk. I grab them and head for the Smoker's Garden. The hotel is empty and skeletal. The colors are fading, the wood cracking, the plaster falling. *Maybe there's been an earthquake,* I think. *No, no. I would have noticed. I think I would have noticed.*

I can smell her perfume in the air. I can feel her presence. She's here like a ghost, they're all here. Everything is here, but everything is gone, and I think *am I real?*

The elevator has never taken so long to ding, and the doors never so long to open. But they do, and the little light flickers like a glowbug. Split Pea, Black Bean. *Christ which is the Smoker's Garden? Fuck it.* I press them all. Mechanical pieces whirl. Ding. Swoosh. Ding Swoosh. Ding. Swoosh. This is it. Smoker's Garden.

I step outside to cold air, pale sun, the aroma of salt and sand. The sweet, sour rotting of dead plants in humidity. They're all wilting and yellow, their heads hanging low in dejection, hiding from the sun, hiding from the wind, lost in a gaze seeing something deep inside the dirt, below the tiles, the concrete, the sand and plaster and plastic, through the layers of wet earth down to the dry bits before the rocks. If the wind stilled, I'd hear a sigh, but the wind spirals, panicked, lost and hurrying to get somewhere, anywhere else.

The longboat is at the edge of the stone wall, tied (halftied) in a careless loop to the fence itself. She floats disinterested and unafraid. *Maybe she'll laugh at me,* I think. But I wade through the beach mud, and the knee-deep water. I flop in in that same unsteady way I did on the tour, hearing Pudge, envisioning Pudge giving that monotone lecture as he holds the boat steady.

I unfasten the craft. Behind the waves, under the clouds, below the feathered gulls, there it is again. It's a loaf of bread, but it looks like a banana floating in the ocean.

The Woman

She's on the train, flying underground, watching her own reflection in glass flashing over brick or concrete that looks black in the unlit tunnel. She studies the shape of her face, how it's changed each day so that she's no longer the image in her head, thinking the world no longer sees the her she knows but some other her that only they know. How it's changed a bit each day, unseen, until one day (she doesn't remember when) it all changed suddenly.

Above her is water or traffic or a city park where people walk dogs, jog. She's been told a portion of the tunnel passes under water. Her elbow rests on her luggage, half guarding it, half supporting the weight of insomnia. When she's not looking at her reflection, she's taking fast glances at other passengers, imagining *their lives imagining lives with them picturing who they go home to if anyone or where they go and what it's like a cat or a dog an old lady boiling meat.*

She sits up, sucking in a deep breath to remind herself *where she's going how she is going home to no one to an empty apartment with dark blue walls* (newly painted) *white tile floors a view of the city center and the people there.* Her dishes will be clean, just as she's left them, there's no one to make a mess, to forget to put away the bread and tempt the ants, to leave a mug of tea on the coffee table. It's as she left it, *it will be.* And she'll roll the luggage in, leave her shoes on the mat inside the door, fall into the sofa, turn on the television and watch whatever it is that everyone is watching these days thinking about tomorrow, tomorrow she'll do the things she needs to do or meant to do or always wanted to do today.

16.

I row out as far as I can go, churning the ocean with wooden oars. The longboat is a ship full of sails. I pump into the nothing. The gray ocean, the gray sky, a distant fog that blurs everything into one nothingness. It seems I'm going nowhere, but the fog overtakes me. If I am in the fog, I'm moving forward, but I'm cold. The color goes and so does warmth.

As everything pulls against me, turns me back, nature herself blows her chill on my skin, numbing my fingers, toes, sending shocks up my arms. I tense and untense my fingers, in and out, but they barely move. I'm not too far to go back. I'm close enough to press on. But the temptation is to stop, to stay in place, to live in this state of cold nothingness where even the thoughts are hard to find.

I have a moment of bilocation. Between my legs, the

155

black case that contains Eduardo Ruiz's invention is simultaneously both the case and a mahogany coffee table. The sensation is like a blurring in and out, or a back and forth, of the two realities at once. All in a single moment, I am rowing the boat, seeing the ocean, the wooden sole, and my cold breath in front of me; and I'm also sipping a hot tea in blue china over the mahogany table, seeing an oriental rug, tropical plants, large windows that offer views of large buildings.

It stops, and I tap the case.

Then I land with a hollow thump on a blank splat of mud that no one would remember, and here I am, on the bread island. Naked, alone, tired, regretful and anxious and ready to go and ready to learn and ready to find something, anything.

"Um, squawk," a naked gull says. "So you're not the usual guy."

"No."

"Hm. Hey, Jimmy. There's a different guy."

"Squawk, how strange. I'll… I guess I'll go let Mr. Delivan know."

"Where's the bread?" another says.

"Bread? I, I didn't bring anything."

"Why not?"

"I, I don't know. I just… I came—"

"You came in the bread boat to the bread island without any bread? This one's a genius. We've got a genius here, guys."

"Did you bring incense? The brass deal to shake it?"

"No, I just came."

"You know, we need that… the bread. You son of a bitch. What are we going to eat? Tuna?"

"It's true, we do," another one says.

"That's what we eat. Look at me, asshole. I don't have any fucking feathers. You think I can catch fish? You think I can order up congee from the waiters? No, I need bread. We all need bread. Mr. Delivan is not going to like this."

"I don't mean to insult you."

"*I don't mean to insult you*," he mimics. "Jimmy, tell Mr. Delivan about the situation we've got up here."

"Sure thing, Dave." Naked Gull Jimmy starts back towards the other end of the dune, but the naked gulls part from the opposite side, face inwards toward each other like you might see at a wedding or a royal ceremony.

"Oh hell, you've done it now," another says to me. "Mr. Delivan almost never comes to this side. Only if there's a big problem. I guess you've done it."

I picture Mr. Delivan in my head like I've done hundreds of times. The way he writes, the words he uses, his voice on the phone. I see a fat man with an angry face, salt-and-pepper hair, a trimmed beard, almost fully receded hairline that he's never given up on and still combs to his right as best as he can, bright-colored collared shirts, boat shoes, artificial tan. Sometimes I see a skinny man, totally bald, with a mustache and sideburns. I have never pictured a naked gull. I've never even seen a naked gull before this

157

trip.

"What's all this? Where's the goddamned bread and incense?" He's several inches taller than the other naked gulls, and he wears a blue scarf.

"Mr. Delivan?"

"I asked you a question, boy." He wiggles his neck in a motion that seems intended to adjust the scarf the way a long-haired person might flick hair out of their face. *'Boy'*? I've never heard him speak that way.

"Mr. Delivan. It's me… I'm… you invited me here." I step backwards. I try to stop, but I keep backing up until the water rises above my boots, starts to fill them.

"Oh. My God. For Christ's sake, kid. Of course. I didn't recognize you. I do now. I'd know that voice anywhere. Did you love the congee? I had it snuck in from China. What the fuck are you doing out here on the island?"

"I'm leaving. I'm trying to leave. You're… I can't—"

"Let's not make this a thing, kid. I'm a bird. You thought I was something else, but I'm not. Now let's move on. Listen, did you love the congee? I was traveling in Southern China, oh that must have been twenty years ago. This old lady—wait, leaving? Where the hell to? You can't leave from here. Not you. Hell, there's a road right there in front of the hotel. You know Andy designed the damn thing, and he thought 'no road.' I said 'listen, Warhol, we're going to need a road if we're expecting guests.' Ain't that right, Andy?"

"I don't remember that. I didn't design the hotel."

158

"Of course you did."

"Jimmy, tell him he designed the hotel."

"You did. I remember it."

"Listen, did you ask the desk for an exit packet? If you want to leave, you have to fill out this exit deal. It's a Customs and Immigration thing. You know, governments. Jesus, here they come." Pedal and Handlebars paddle toward us in a tandem kayak, also bright red.

"There's no way out that way."

"Well, did you turn in the packet?"

"It's… I'm still working on it." I'm using all my strength to not look at the longboat, where the device is. A glance into the boat would reveal it.

"So get back to work, kid. Otherwise just wait. Your reservation will be up soon enough."

"I've given up on all that. I'm done with all of this. I'm ready to be gone," I say. "I'll paddle this damn boat across the ocean at this point." I move forward, back onto the dune where the water only reaches up to my ankles.

"Alright. Let's not get all dramatic. Frankly, I'm surprised you wouldn't want to stay."

"Ahoy, gentlemen," Pedal shouts. "We're searching for the man with the device, Mr. Edu—"

"Not now, idiots." Mr. Delivan waves them away.

"Do not inter—"

"I said not now, idiots. Christ." I have to blink my eyes about half a dozen times. I'm certain Handlebars tucked an actual tail between his legs before defeatedly lowering his

159

paddle.

"I appreciate the hospitality, the invitation. Everything. It's just, I'm ready to get back."

"If that's the case then, do me a favor."

"What's that?"

"Give me and Jimmy a ride back in. To the Smoker's Garden. This way we don't have to wait around for the fat kid to bring more bread and incense."

"I'd rather keep going." There are lights far ahead at the edge of the horizon. Lights that say a shining city is waiting for me, lights that blink with the passing waves. Puffs of smoke, which I can only imagine are chimneys, rise to the sky like rain clouds. It's freedom there in the sunrise. "I'm sure he'll be by with the bread soon."

"How's he going to get here without the damn boat?"

"I brought something else."

"Oh hell."

"Yes, the feather machine." I pull it out from the long-boat. The black case sucks in light and maybe even sound. The water splashes, but the case stays dry. It's as if there is a tear in reality. It's not really black, it is nothing. It is the absence of light with a chrome buckle.

"Oh God," several of the birds say.

"It's more valuable, more important," I say. "And it's yours to do with as you see fit."

"We need to sit down."

"Get off our island with that witchcraft," Jimmy yells. He stomps his feet, splashing me.

"No. He's right. This is it," Mr. Delivan says. "All we do is stall, but this is it. Take out the contraption."

"No, Mr. Delivan, no, sir. This isn't a good idea," Jimmy says.

"It's time. Get it out, kid. Set it up." The naked gulls move away, little by little, to the edges of the dune as far away as they can get from us. I bring the case from the boat, open the box, and start to set it up the way I'd seen Eduardo do it.

"We're here now," I said. "That place where we ask that strange question…"

"And what is the strange question?" His eyes are fixed to the contraption while I twist the long pipe into the tripod. The other gulls, following Jimmy's lead, turn their backs to us. They're weeping.

"It's… 'what are you?'"

"Is that the question? What everyone wonders back in life?"

"It is."

"It's simple." He lowers his body into the water so that he's floating like a duck. "We are the forgotten dead, the roaming spirits. The ones who died alone or died with nothing or, in some cases, with everything. But we are cursed, or maybe we're damned. When our eyes looked to Heaven we prayed: 'God give us wings to reach Your Kingdom.' Metaphorically, I mean. I'm an atheist. That is how I like to see it."

"I'm born-again," Jimmy says.

161

"Yes, Jimmy, we've heard it."

"We've heard it alright," another gull adds.

"We're stuck between realities. Just tell him."

"It's more complicated than that."

"We were humans in this reality. I guess we are birds in another, but we're stuck in the wrong place."

"Like reincarnation?" I ask.

"No, not like reincarnation."

"But you're dead?"

"Well, not really. Jesus, listen. We're not dead. I like to say the forgotten dead thing because it sounds cool. We are humans in this reality. We are birds in our assigned reality. Something got mixed up, and we're in the wrong places at the same time. So here we are the lost spirits and the forgotten dead, but also we don't exist here because we are alive and happy somewhere else."

"But that's Andy Warhol, right?"

"And?"

"He's dead."

"No, he's not dead. You're just in the wrong place."

"I don't think I understand," I say.

"If everyone will excuse me," Mr. Delivan quiets the fuss. "The truth is, we had the wings all along. We all do, but birds don't just need wings to fly, they need feathers too, and what is a bird without feathers? A naked gull waddling along the shore, waiting for the afterlife, not flying, not fishing, eating charity bread, and dodging crocodiles."

"It's not the afterlife," someone mumbles.

"Will you quiet down now?"

"How long do you stay here, like this?" I ask.

"I don't know. Maybe forever. Maybe never. We don't know where we came from, who we were. We only know we are here. As far as any of us can remember, this is where we've always been, how we've always been. It's possible we were never here at all, or that we're only here so long as we dodge the crocodiles. There is no life after the crocodile."

"I remember being human."

"As far as any of us can remember, this is how it's always been."

"So, you're all dead? Ghosts?"

"No. We're, how can I explain this, kid? We're no longer part of the same reality as you, but we are trapped between, we'll say 'dimensions,' I guess. I don't like to use that word, though, kid. I don't want to get all sci-fi about it."

"You're kidding. That's what I've been trying to say."

"I think we're in purgatory," Jimmy says.

"Not now, Jimmy. We're trying to hear," another gull says.

"Our realities have different rules. We are stuck between yours and ours. That's all. Nothing more complicated than that."

"I suppose we agree on that."

"So what happens next?" I cross my legs and lower myself into the water. We, Mr. Delivan and I, are both sitting.

"Next, the best I can figure, kid, is you load us into that machine, one by one, and you launch us off. Some of us will fly away, joining the other gulls with our wings. We will follow our instinct to wherever it is we're supposed to go."

"It's that way," Jimmy says, staring off into the distance.

"Some of us won't. When you're done, and we're gone, the feathered gulls, which have been too afraid to leave us behind, will stop flying in their pattern and move on too. And that leaves you, you and that hotel chasing you towards the horizon."

THE END

Learn more at **WordRebels.com**

Word Rebels, LLC
506 N. Bishop Ave
Dallas, TX 75208

Thank you for reading *Naked Gulls.* I wrote most of this novel over a few months in Mexico. It started out as a bizarre dream, some of which was too bizarre to put in the final draft, but I do hope I left enough weird in it to give you something interesting.

This novel ultimately led to my founding Word Rebels Press with the straighforward mission of creating an independent literary press that supports independent bookstores. If you'd like to get involved or learn more about Word Rebels Press and/or my previous and forthcoming release please visit WordRebels.com.

Thanks again,

Marco

P.S. Please don't hestitate to reach out to me on social media @RealMarcoCavazos or by email at MarcosCavazos@yahoo.com.